DIGITAL DECEPTION

A PARKER PHOTOGRAPHY COZY MYSTERY

SUZANNE BOLDEN

LAUGHING DEER PRESS

CONTENTS

A professional movie production team had never set foot in Harmony. Excitement among the residents was palpable!

We saw our share of politicians come to town and film campaign ads. After all, Harmony offered a traditional small town on the river vibe for the background, salt of the earth people to showcase, and cute babies to kiss. A sure-fire way to appeal to voters.

The Ace hardware store filmed testimonials of customers once and had a Greensville ad agency put them into a commercial. Val's son Travis did a commercial with his two sons when he opened the Harris and Sons Marine Maintenance business outside of town. A large crowd gathered to watch that, while many of the boys' friends teased and made faces at them during the filming. And when the Stone Mill Brewery completed their outdoor patio, they promoted it on our area stations to attract customers from across the Driftless area.

But this was different! A full-length movie, based on the memoir of a well-known soap opera actress, and featuring Harmony. This was global, everyone said. It would put us on the map. I'm not sure what map we were missing from, but now we would be on it.

The location scouting trip by Beverly Turner's daughter Alli was the first inkling we'd gotten that this movie was happening. Through papers left behind by her adoptive parents, Alli discovered her mother's biological father, Josiah Bell. She learned that he lived in Harmony, Wisconsin. Plans were put in place to film a short segment of the story of Beverly's life here in our town.

It was on her second trip to Harmony that more pieces fell into place, and she found out that Joanna Parker, my mother, was also Beverly's mother. The evening Alli introduced me to Beverly was the most shocking moment of my life. I had a half-sister! Our mother named both her daughters after Kennedy women. Me after Jacqueline and Beverly, whose birth name was Caroline, after Jackie Kennedy's daughter.

With that revelation came the hurt of knowing my

mother Joanna had been unfaithful to my father. Now the story of her affair would be on the big screen for all to see. I could only imagine the comments from Harmony residents when the movie came out, and they realized what they were witnessing. Two locals, the onetime owner of the high-end dress shop Vogue on Main and a well-respected judge, had a dalliance that resulted in a pregnancy.

The couple in Florida who adopted the little baby kept the name given to her by her mother. They never told Caroline she was adopted. But as so often happens, she eventually found out that she'd been given up at birth. Hurt and angry at being kept in the dark, she broke off relations with her adoptive parents and fled to New York City to pursue her dreams. Her passion was theater. She wanted to be an actress. So, she left Florida for the bright lights of Broadway right after graduating high school.

Later in life, she found herself filled with regrets over how she'd treated her family about their decision to keep the adoption from her. After all, the couple had raised her and loved her wholeheartedly. Caroline decided to honor her adoptive mother by taking her first name, Beverly. Thus, the name of her memoir, *Becoming Beverly*.

But none of Alli's, Wade's, or Beverly's visits

prepared us for the Hollywood circus that descended on Harmony yesterday. Three large semi trucks with unmarked white trailers arrived and were directed to park on the side streets behind the Village Hall. Vans transporting film crew from the airport in Milwaukee arrived at the Riverview Motel and Cottages. Several other members of the production drove rental cars and stayed at the Whitlow Bed and Breakfast, originally the home of Judge Bell and his wife, Mary.

I peered out the front window of Parker Photography Studio and Gallery this morning to watch the hustle and bustle of activity on Main Street as it was being prepped for filming.

"How do they do this so fast?" Mandy, my employee and the daughter-in-law of my sweetie, asked. "Check out Sutton Antiques. It's already back to looking like the pictures from decades ago when your mom's dress shop was there. Does it look the same?"

"It does," I said, thinking how eerie it was to see Vogue on Main brought back to life. "I can't wait for Aunt Ruth to see this. She'll get a kick out of the automobiles from the 50s they've lined the street with. She tells the funniest stories of Mom and her learning to drive. Didn't Alli ask you to take social media and promotional photographs?"

"Oh my gosh. Yes. I can't believe I almost forgot. I

even have an official title. Unit photographer. I'd better get out there and start snapping. She's going to want to post photos of the progress here every day."

"I've been watching her Instagram account since she first told me about making this movie," I said. "Do you get to decide which photographs to post?"

"No, I just get them resized for different media and write a quick note about the shot. Then Alli or her assistant director will post which one they want."

"Todd, I think you should volunteer to help with the blurbs. You have a skill with words and media experience through your blog and in your magazine articles."

Todd Baldwin, a young friend from Chicago, had come to Harmony to visit. He agreed to stay and help me when I took over Parker Photography from my Aunt Ruth.

"You'll get to be around Alli more," Mandy teased as she gathered up her camera.

"Yep," Todd said. "That crossed my mind. Maybe I could write samples on your photographs before you forward them to her?"

"Good idea. Alli's got her plate full as director. She might welcome one less thing to manage," Mandy said.

Old-fashioned parking meters with penny coin slots appeared on Main Street. Luckily our new streetlamps were modeled after the ones from days gone by, so they fit perfectly with the styling the film required.

A yellow and white striped awning being put up looked just like the one I remember from childhood. A sign with elegant black script lettering spelling out Vogue on Main now hung across the storefront, obscuring the Sutton Antiques sign. Our historical society had worked with Patti Hunt, the village administrator, to keep the original authentic feeling to Main Street. Buildings along the street kept basically the same look as when they were built. Some business owners grumbled about the restrictions, but the continuity and historic feeling proved to be appreciated and admired by tourists. Alli had said they wouldn't spend a ton of time on the exteriors, as covering up signs and taking off entire additions could be changed digitally in the editing process. The magic of Hollywood.

I watched Mandy rest her camera on the antique parking meter to take some shots of the facade changes being made. Then she disappeared inside, where the interior set designer would be busy at work, transforming an antique store into a dress shop.

I tried to ignore the weird feelings I was having seeing my mother's dress shop come back to life. After she passed on, no one took the business over. Besides, by that time, most of the women who had shopped there were going to big city stores like Marshall Fields in Chicago or Gimbel's in Milwaukee.

"Can you believe all this? I'm so excited," Kirsten said, as she pushed through the front door. The granddaughter of a friend, she worked here part time as she earned her online degree. The flexible hours I offered her were perfect.

Right now, I was grateful for the distraction. I was bracing for more feelings flooding over me in the next few days, but they'd come when they would. "Morning, Kirsten. I'm doing good. The film people will come in to make some tweaks to our place today. I want you and Todd to move all our display panels into the back and take down the photographs hanging on the wall. Scott helped me to move the bigger things yesterday, so you should be able to manage."

"Will do. I looked up the title for the person who designs the set. Art director. I'm going to meet a real Hollywood person," Kirsten said. "I wonder if they'll have a construction coordinator and gaffer and grips and..."

"Whoa, Kirsten," Todd said. "You did your research, but I'm not sure you'll get to use all those titles here. Alli is running a small budget production. There might be just a couple of people making the changes. They're working across the street at Sutton's now."

"I'm going over to take a peek at the progress. Kirsten, do you know if your grandmother is coming in later to be an extra?"

"She is. Grandma Dorothy and her Shady Pines friends are dressing in clothes fit for the era. Do you believe they even still have those? I mean, that had to be forever ago. Were you like a toddler then?"

Ah, the perspective of a teenager, I thought. "No, in fact, I was just a little younger than you during the time this film represents."

"Is it like too weird to see that antique shop being changed back to your mom's dress shop?"

"It is very strange. Time travel vibe to it."

"Are you going by to try out for an extra part?" Todd asked me.

"I already have a small part," I said with a wink. "Remember, the director is my niece. Plus, she promised to put Libby in the movie too."

"No lines for Libby, though?" Todd laughed.

CHAPTER TWO

crossed the street to peek in the windows and check out the interior redo of Sutton's Antiques, taking it back to Vogue on Main. Hannah and Mark Sutton kept the beautiful wooden trim work when they took over the empty space. The dark walnut wood in the wainscoting and coffered ceiling detail, along with the original front counter, was untouched.

Hannah came hurrying out when she saw me at the window. "This is so cool. The transformation process is unbelievable. They've already moved all the big pieces. With the payment for this weeklong lease, Mark and I can take a nice vacation."

"Wow, nice. Any plans on where you might go?"

"I'd like to do an island in the Caribbean in January. Something warm and sunny when the bitter days of winter hit," Hannah said. "But seeing the props they brought in is making me itchy to do an antique hunting trip out East."

"Any spooky mannequins show up?" I asked. "I remember the creeps they gave me when I was little."

Hannah pointed to mannequins being moved from the back and placed in the front display windows. "Are those what you mean?"

"Oh yeah! Those are exactly like the ones I hated. Very strange looking to a kid. Especially when Mom closed for the day and turned out the lights. Their eyes seemed to follow me."

The dresses being put on the mannequins were styles I remembered. Women in town admired my mother's taste in fashion. They waited with anticipation for the new garments and accessories, arriving after one of her buying trips to New York or Los Angeles. I watched from our photography studio across the street as women strolled by Vogue on Main, slowing down to see what was on display. Mom rotated the dresses and accessories. One week she might center it on soft cream trousers and blazers with saddle leather flats. She'd stage the display with a Hermes scarf draped over the handbag on the mannequin's arm. The picnic theme displayed a straw hamper and checkered cloth spread on the display window floor. It featured white capris on all the mannequins with different vivid colored summer tops and sunglasses to cover their empty eyes. In fall she scattered colorful leaves around to accent the rich tones of autumn in plaid woolen jackets over deep rust sheaths. I was remembering how I loved the window display with the jewel toned evening dresses and the peacock feathers lining the window's edge when my thoughts were interrupted.

"Jackie. Hey Jackie. I lost you. Where did your mind just take you?" Hannah asked.

I sighed and smiled at my friend. "Sorry. I was back in time. My mother used to do the most beautiful window displays. I was just caught up in the memories. What were you saying?"

"Ah, that's sweet. I've heard this was quite the place. But what I was pointing out was that the clothes they brought in for the filming are amazing. And the bags and shoes are perfect. I hope they do your mother's memory justice. Hey, that reminds me." Hannah reached into her pocket and pulled out business cards. "Here, I knew you'd want one."

I looked down at what she handed me. It was a card that read Vogue on Main and the tagline, *Where women of style shop*! The card included my mother's original black and white logo of a strolling woman stylishly represented by a few simple black strokes.

"They have shopping bags too. I'm going to grab some when they are done shooting. Want me to save one for you too?"

"Ah yeah, sure," I murmured.

"Jackie, is something wrong?" Hannah asked.

I smiled. "No. Not really. Just feeling a little sad. Guess you never get over missing your parents."

Hannah squeezed my arm. "I'm heading over to the Village Hall to check how Patti is doing. Want to come with?"

The original stone building of our Village Hall grounded the village square on the west, with the river and marina forming its southern border. This lovely green space was now sprinkled with the spring colors of daffodils, tulips, and hyacinths. Green shoots told of daylilies waiting their turn to bloom. They had tastefully added on to the municipal building as Harmony grew. Village offices, along with the library, our police station, and post office all surrounded the park.

The planning that had to go into even a small independent film was breathtaking. Because of its central location, Alli worked with Patti to use basement rooms in the Village Hall for offices, dressing rooms, and film editing. The ground floor multipurpose room with its waxed pine floors and small stage solved the need for a common gathering area. Here, crew members and performers found information about daily happenings.

The community used the low-ceilinged basement's warren of rooms for a variety of things like Boy and Girl Scout meetings, Mommy and Me classes, and Monday night bingo. That's where we found Patti.

"Hey guys. Can you make sure you're not over-loading the circuits? The electrical panel is right back there," Patti called out to someone we couldn't see. She stepped out of the way as people scurried by carrying equipment, computers, and stacks of paper. Everyone seemed focused and efficient, appearing to know just what needed doing.

"Hey Jackie! Over here."

I'd recognize that voice anywhere. Kim Walters leaned out of a doorway. She was much more than our local real estate agent extraordinaire. She involved herself in innumerable and diverse events across the community. Now here she stood, cool and calm in the middle of this swirl. The brown and cream chevrons in her fitted dress complimented her chestnut hair and her makeup was, as usual, perfect.

"This way. I'd like you to meet someone."

Hannah and I entered what appeared to be a dressing

room. Suits and shirts hung on a rolling rack. A mirrored dressing table stood against one wall. They had hung a curtain across the room and a peek to the other side showed a similarly arranged area.

"They moved the primary stars' dressing areas here instead of the big old trailer outside. Isn't it cool?" Kim said. "Mandy was just here to take some photographs. Stu is going to do a big wrap-up article in the next Harmony Happenings. I can't believe this is really coming to life after all this time. Just think, I was in on it from the very beginning."

"That's true, you were Kim. But who did you want us to meet?" Hannah asked.

A flamboyantly handsome man stepped from the other side of the curtain. "I assume Kim meant me."

"Rod, this is Hannah Sutton and Jacqueline Parker."

He extended his hand. "I'm Rod Jessup, also known as Josiah Bell for this movie. Nice to meet you. Am I hearing this right? Are you the actual daughter of Dionne?"

My puzzled expression prompted a quick explanation from Kim. "Dionne is the actress playing your mother, Jackie. And the other male dressing area is going to be used by your father. I haven't met him yet."

"Nice to meet you, Mr. Jessup. I hope you can tell how very excited we are," Hannah said.

Alli poked her head in. "Rod, have you seen Wade?"

"He was over in the editing room last time I saw him," Rod answered.

"Oh, hi Jackie, I didn't know you were here. It was so nice to catch up last night. Will you be out at Stone Mill later?" Alli asked in a hurried voice.

"I'm not sure. What's going on there?"

"A welcome to Harmony gathering for our group. Please come, we'd love to have you. Ruth is planning on coming too. We want the cast to meet the people who were part of Beverly's story." And with that, she was gone.

"I'm going for sure," Kim said. "I would have thought you saw the email about it. I think it's on the call sheet too. Or posted on the board upstairs."

"Email? Call sheet?"

"Jackie, you must get with it." Kim snapped her fingers in the air. "Things move fast around here."

Rod gave a low chuckle. "The call sheet is just a schedule for the day. Not a term everyone knows. There are many moving parts to filming and a talented director keeps things like that organized. Ms. Turner is trying, but might be feeling overwhelmed. Her father, Dennis, is the ghost director. He has her back."

"Alli and I met up briefly last night when she got to town," I said. "Just got in a quick hello when she arrived at my friend's bed and breakfast. Has Beverly gotten in yet?"

Kim shook her head. "I don't think so. I have the sense this part of the filming will be hard for her. Rod told me she didn't show up at the site in New York, either. Strange she wouldn't be there to show support for Alli. Course she might be avoiding her ex-husband, Dennis."

"I thought their divorce was amicable."

Rod shrugged. "Sure. Right. That's what they all like to say. Hollywood can be a small town. Lots of complicated relationships in the movie industry."

"I've been following Instagram posts to keep up with what's going on," I said. "Looks like it's been exciting. But why were you and Dionne on the New York site? Your characters lived here."

"Just quick in and out scenes in New York for myself and Dionne. Apparently, your mother and I carried on most of our affair out of the sight of Harmony. New York and LA hosted the clothing marts Joanna Parker went to on her buying trips. And I," Rod said with a lascivious wink, "would make excuses to show up there at the same time."

The stab in my heart burned.

Rod noticed my strange reaction. "I'm sorry. Was that being cruel?"

Hannah gently rested her hand on my arm.

I took a deep breath. "Just caught me wrong, Rod. I'm still adjusting to knowing I have a half-sister. Guess I don't like to think about what my mother did to make that happen."

"Of course. I wasn't thinking," Rod said. "I was flippant and trying to be cute."

"And you are cute," Kim said. "Come on, Jackie. Let me show you around some more. We'll see you later, Judge Bell."

Kim was filled with knowledge of what was being set up in these rooms. We toured Dionne's dressing area. There we met Laura, the film's costume designer. In the largest room, Kim pointed out a screen for viewing the outtakes from each day of filming. Across the room I noticed computer towers and multiple screens set up for film editing. Alli, Wade Lambert, and another man were in a deep discussion.

"Ooh, I think that's Dennis, Alli's father," Kim whispered. "I've been dying to meet him."

Hannah grabbed her arm as she started in. "They're busy. Later. Let's head back upstairs."

Patti joined us in the multipurpose room. "Getting the tour, I see. Kim has been invaluable in helping everyone navigate. It was her idea to help sponsor the gathering at the Stone Mill tonight. We want it to be a friendly welcome to Harmony for the cast and crew. Benny, the manager there, is onboard and giving us special rates. We're all grateful to this gal for making it happen."

Kim brushed off the compliments with a flip of her hand. "No problem, Patti. I love the vibes here. Lights. Camera. Action. And I get a speaking part in the film. Can you believe it? I'm going to be a clerk in Vogue on Main." Kim straightened her shoulders and turned her head to one side. "I hope they shoot from my best angle and with good lighting."

"So, what are your lines? In fact, what are my lines?" I asked.

Patti handed me a script from the pile resting on a table. "They start on page 35 and end on page 36."

I drew back with a hand on my chest. "Will I be able to handle that?"

Kim laughed. "Hey, we all must start somewhere. See you two later at the Stone Mill." Kim pulled her sunglasses out of her bag, put them on, and strode out the front door of the Village Hall, almost bumping into someone rolling a rack of clothes in. The wardrobe person easily steered it around Kim while she slipped past and out the front entry.

The woman pushing the rack asked, "Dionne's dressing room?"

Patti pointed her downstairs. Within a second, someone grabbed the other end of the rack and he easily lifted it, helping get it down to the basement. As soon as the rack cleared the steps, three people came hurrying up and headed out the front door.

"Grand Central Station," Hannah said.

"So, I can keep this script as a souvenir?" I asked.

"Check it out," Patti said, pointing to the top corner of the front cover where I read *Jacqueline Parker shopper*. "It's all yours. Since you have a speaking part, Alli's getting you a SAG card. Another souvenir."

"SAG?"

"Screen Actors Guild," Alli said as she came up from the lower level. "Even a small speaking part means you can join the union. I thought you might get a kick out of that."

"But I don't act. What could I say? It says I'm a shopper. I'm not even a good shopper!"

A tall, handsome man, his black hair streaked with the perfect amount of gray around the temple, joined us. It was the man who'd been in the editing room with her. "The pay isn't the best, but according to Alli, that won't concern you as I understand you are a world-famous photographer. Please let me introduce myself, Dennis Turner.

He extended his hand and took mine, holding it

lightly. "It is indeed a pleasure to meet you, Jackie. Now, if Bev and I had not divorced, I believe you'd be my sister-in-law. Or half something?"

His charming grin held my attention. "I'm delighted to meet you, Mr. Turner."

"Please. Call me Dennis."

"As for the half, how about we drop that? I consider Alli my niece and you my…"

"Ex brother-in-law? Ah, things get complicated. How about we just call each other friends?" Dennis gently released my hand and turned to Patti.

"We are having some concerns about humidity in the basement. Do you have dehumidifiers available?"

"We might," Patti said with hesitation. "I'll see what I can scrounge up."

"Scott's construction sites have dehumidifiers on them. I might be able to get a couple for you from him."

"Of course," Patti said. "Great thought, Jackie."

Dennis tilted his head and smiled. "Friend? Good friend?"

"Daddy!" Alli scolded as she punched him on the shoulder. "Scott is Jackie's boyfriend. Now stop with the flirting. Jackie, I will apologize in advance for my father's way with women."

Rubbing his arm, Dennis grinned. "Ouch, my little

one. I'm an unapologetic appreciator of women. Will we see you at the gathering tonight, Jackie?"

"Yes, and I'll be with my Aunt Ruth."

"The night I met her was special. I'll never forget it. I told you about it, Daddy. It was the night Mom learned who her birth mother was and met her family. I tried contacting the Bell relatives but was stonewalled," Alli said.

"I remember you talking about that. Quite excited you were. Isn't the B&B we're staying at where Bev's father lived?"

"It is," Alli said. "I won't make the start of the party. My to-do list keeps growing. But I can guarantee I will be there at some point."

Before stepping out the door, Dennis said, "I plan on showing up early and look forward to seeing you tonight."

CHAPTER THREE

I was disappointed Scott couldn't make it to the party tonight, but it was for a good reason. He was being presented with one of the annual awards the Southwest Wisconsin Homebuilder's group presented to their members. Because of his construction company's involvement with many of the new homes being built on The Hills resort grounds, Scott was rising in prominence in this entire part of the state.

Scott was disappointed, too. I would have loved to be there to see him receive the award, but I thought it important to be at the Stone Mill tonight to represent the Parker family. I hoped he wasn't upset about it.

Patti called me earlier to thank me for suggesting the construction dehumidifiers. Turns out that Scott's construction crew delivered three dehumidifiers to the

Village Hall and now they were all set to fight the humidity that builds up in old basements.

"Scott's such a good guy," Patti said. "I should know. I married him once!"

Scott and Patti's marriage ended in divorce over thirty years ago, but that didn't interfere with their life here in Harmony. They both shared grandparenting joys with Mandy and Matt's little boy, Ty. Patti's husband was a local attorney, but Scott never remarried. Things don't always go that way, but here it was true. Divorce could be amicable.

"I'm a lucky lady to call him my sweetie," I told her. I still hadn't found the right word to describe our relationship. Both of us were in our sixties, so boyfriend and girlfriend sounded too young. Sweetie seemed like good enough for now. Would we be something more one day?

Aunt Ruth and I walked up to the front door of the Stone Mill Brewery as a van with the logo of my friend Wanda's Riverview Motel, usually used to shuttle people to local airports or the Amtrak train station in Portage, pulled up. Young people spilled out, teasing and jostling, looking forward to drinks and food after putting in a long day.

"I'm excited they invited us to this gathering," Ruth said.

"I'm grateful you came, so I have someone to hang out with."

"Didn't Scott have that big event in Greensville tonight?"

"Yeah. I feel bad missing it," I said, holding the door open for the arriving group.

"I didn't know how many people it takes to make a movie. Even a low budget one. What do they all do?"

But before I could answer, we saw Benny, the manager of the Stone Mill, and Stuart Walters wave to us from across the pub. Behind them, heat lamps glowed on the patio. Spring nights got chilly here by the river.

"Ruth, let's go grab a barstool by Stuart and Benny if we can."

"I'm with you. I like to keep my head above the crowd and not be that little old lady sitting down at a table all night, waiting to see who will choose to sit and visit with her."

"Ruth, come on. You are not that little old lady type."

"That's because I'm usually with my Shady Pines friends, so we present a united front. Kay was supposed to bring Granny G tonight, but I don't see her yet."

"I know why we were invited, but why them?" I said. "Oops, that sounded weird. I mean, what connection do they have to this event?"

"Don't you remember? Granny G used to work for

the Judge and Mary Bell around the time all this stuff hit the fan," Ruth said. "She wanted to bring Kay along as a companion. They've struck up a close friendship. Kay has no other relatives in town. Grannie G either. Plus, Kay's B&B is where some of the movie people are staying."

Stu reached to steady Ruth as she sat up on a barstool. "Quite a soiree my wife threw," Stu said proudly. "Kim is out working the crowd."

"Did you meet any of the actors?" I asked.

"I met Dionne Stockton, who is playing your mother, Jackie. Stunning woman, just like Joanna was."

"You never met my mother, did you?" I asked, trying to place things and people on a timeline.

"I didn't, but I've seen her photographs. A gorgeous woman."

"Have you met the man playing my brother, Bob?" Ruth asked.

"I have not," Stu said, pulling a small notecard out of his pocket and reading, "Shayne Givens is his name."

"A cheat sheet, Stu? Might be a smart move," I said.

"It is. I know they like to imagine we all know who they are. Famous people and all that," Stu said.

"Stu, I don't know if they are so famous. Maybe the man playing Judge Bell," Benny said. "I've seen him in some movies and TV. And that young actress playing you, Jackie. My daughter said she knows her from a Disney movie."

"Bella Cameron. Fifteen years old." Stuart raised himself up on his toes to scan the crowd. "Oh, and there's the famous cinematographer, Lewis Berry. He's won an academy award."

"Wasn't Dennis Turner also a winner once?" Benny asked. "He's supposed to be here tonight, too."

Stu shrugged. "I think just a nominee. But I loved the Westerns he directed."

"Aunt Ruth, if you're okay here I'd like to take a stroll around the room."

"I'm good. Keep your eyes open for Granny G and Kay for me."

The crowd seemed to enjoy themselves. That made me happy. Happy crew…happy movie making…happy Harmony.

I stopped to say hi to Mandy, who was busy getting photographs of everyone. "Glad to see you're taking your job seriously. Do you have to get releases to post these photographs?"

"I hope not! Alli or Wade will handle that. Give me a pose, Jackie. Let me play paparazzi."

"Okay, I can get into that." I took my hand-printed scarf and tossed it teasingly over my shoulder, dipping my head and turning toward Mandy's camera.

She pretended to move around me as though I was a famous movie star. I kept on posing. Peeked over my shoulder. A chin up worldly gaze. Next teasing lips slightly parted touched by one finger pose.

We both burst out laughing.

"Got some good ones," Mandy said.

"Do not share those with Wade or Alli," I warned.

"How about with Scott?"

"That would be okay." I turned to walk away and crashed right into Dennis Turner's chest.

He took me in his arms and whispered, "Sorry I'm late. Darn time differences mean I do business when I'd rather be here having fun." Then he spun back toward the camera to continue the pretend charade with Mandy.

"Going Hollywood on us, Jackie?" Kay asked as she guided Granny G past us.

"Yeah right," I said, grabbing the chance to pull away from Dennis. "Ruth is looking for you. She's sitting at the bar by Stuart."

"Let her know Patti and Charlie are saving us a seat outside on the patio," Kay said. "I hope they cranked up the heat lamps."

"I want to meet the actors playing the Judge and Mary Bell. That's my only aim tonight," Granny G said.

Dennis turned to a woman standing nearby. Young,

with a terrific figure hugged by a tight blue sequined dress, the woman's face showed she was out of sorts.

"Eleana, would you be a doll and find Rod? This lovely woman wants to meet him. Tell him I sent you and that she'll be on the patio."

Dennis turned back to Grannie G. "I haven't seen the actress portraying the Judge's wife. But Eleana will get Rod Jessup and find you on the patio."

Behind Dennis's back I watched a disdainful look cross Eleana's sullen face. She faked a smile and said, "Of course." She spun on her tall heels and walked away with her head held high.

CHAPTER FOUR

*D*ennis took Granny G's arm. "May I have the pleasure of walking you out to the patio while my assistant hunts down Mr. Jessup?"

Granny G patted Dennis's hand. "Of course. Thank you."

Kay walked with me as she distanced us from Dennis. "That was awkward," Kay said. "Eleana only became his assistant last night. When they all arrived at my place yesterday trouble was brewing."

"Who's staying at your B&B?"

"Alli, and her father. Marta, the film editor. Wade Lambert was booked together with his girlfriend Eleana. Shortly after they arrived, Alli asked if I had another room available. She told me Eleana was in her room crying and saying she couldn't stay with Wade. I had a free room because Beverly canceled her booking saying she'd rather stay somewhere else. She didn't want to run into her ex in the hall. I pointed her towards The Hills resort because I think Wanda's Riverview Motel was filled up with the rest of the crew."

"Oh boy. Not a good start for their time here."

"Agreed. I overheard Dennis tell Eleana she could stay on as his assistant if she wanted so it would cover her expenses for the next few days. They'll all be flying back to LA after filming here is completed."

They had strung patio lights around the perimeter and crossing over the center of the deck. On the river below a pontoon had just docked and guests were coming up the steps to the Stone Mill's patio. They seemed to be part of the film crew by the greetings that were called out to them.

We made it to Charlie and Patti Hunt's table. Dennis helped Granny G to her chair, but then excused himself saying he was expecting someone who'd be arriving on the pontoon.

"Did you arrange for the river taxi?" I asked Patti. "Nice idea."

"I did. They had a brief tour of Lake Harmony before arriving here. Only bad thing was that I needed a fill-in because the pontoon which I was going to use had last minute engine trouble. Matt agreed to help out, though he needs to get to his father's award ceremony tonight. He said he can race over there and catch the presentation part of the evening after he gets back to the marina."

Matt came walking up behind the guests he'd brought over. "Hi Mom. They enjoyed the boat ride. Did a little partying and cruising around Lake Harmony, but then the sun set and bam! Cold. Good thing I threw some blankets on earlier. I told them all I'm off duty now and they can catch the shuttle back to the Riverview. Okay with you?"

"Of course. I was just telling Jackie that you got roped into helping me. Looks like you'll be able to make it to your dad's event," Patti said.

Mandy came up with a steaming cup of coffee for Matt. "Here you go, honey. Have this before you race off into the night."

Dennis stepped up and casually put his arm around my waist. The gesture startled me and caught Matt's attention as well.

"Say, young man, was Wade Lambert on your pontoon boat?"

"I don't believe so, sir."

Again, I had to extricate myself from Dennis Turner's grasp. "I wish Scott had made it here. But I'm so happy you'll be there to see him get the award," I said.

"Ah yeah. Me too." Matt gave me a questioning look, before kissing Mandy's cheek. "Thanks for the coffee. I'm going over to say a quick hi to Dave and then take off. I'll see you at home later."

One more glance at me over his shoulder made me feel even worse. What would he say to Scott?

Eleana came walking up with Rod Jessup in tow. "Here you go. Job completed."

Dennis shot her a stern look. "Are you aware Wade hasn't arrived?"

With a smile pasted on her face Eleana said, "I wasn't aware. And I don't care. Do you?"

"I do. I wanted to talk to him. But it can wait." Dennis introduced Rod to Granny G before excusing himself.

By the look on her face, I could see Granny was in awe. "I know you. You were the bar owner in…oh darn, I can't put my finger on the show's name. It used to be on Thursday nights."

"*The Neighbors?*" Rod offered.

"That's it! You were great. Can I get your autograph?" she asked.

"Oh course. I'd be honored. Will you be on set tomorrow? The casting call has me filming at the Bell mansion in the morning."

"I hope I can get there. This is the woman who owns

the house, Kay Whitlow. She's made it a bed and breakfast. Looks just like when I worked there. Wait until I tell the kids I met you."

I waved Mandy over to get a photograph of Granny G and Rod together.

"I'll print this and have a copy for you to sign in the morning," Mandy said.

"Nice to see you again, Jackie," Rod said. "I hope you're enjoying the party despite Dennis' misbehavior. I feel I must apologize for those of my gender who think they can put their hands all over a lady. But I will say he recognizes beauty when he sees it."

"Thank you, Rod. I've got his number. I can handle him."

"Call if you need any help," Rod said. With a small bow, he excused himself.

Granny G wanting to meet the actor playing Judge Bell put an idea in my head that Ruth might like to meet the actress playing her sister-in-law Joanna. Stu said Dionne was here. Oh, and the actor playing her brother too. I looked forward to seeing them myself. My mother and my father. Would it feel odd?

But how to find them? I didn't want to ask Dennis. But I saw Eleana and decided she could help me. She was talking with someone at the bar nearby. As I approached them, I heard her low, angry voice directed at one of the crew who arrived on Matt's pontoon boat.

Eleana leaned in to grill the young man who was trying to order a drink at the bar. "So where did he go?"

"I don't know. He's your boyfriend. You keep tabs on him yourself."

Eleana glared at him. "He's not my boyfriend anymore. Stop calling him that. Is he with someone else tonight? Who?"

"Look, Eleana. I don't want to get in the middle of this. I've learned to stay far away from all the love triangles, affairs, and divorces. Keep me out of it!" He spun, bumped into me, and sloshed his beer on Eleana's blue dress.

"Sorry. Didn't see you there," he mumbled.

Benny jumped in, reaching for clean towels the bartender handed him and began to wipe the beer off Eleanor.

"Stop it. I'll get it myself. Get away from me." She snatched the towels from Benny's hands and roughly patted the liquid off her sequins.

By this point I knew it wouldn't be a good time to ask Eleana anything. I glanced in her direction. She bugged out her eyes back at me. I tried a smile, but it only produced one word from her.

"What?" She threw the towels down on the bar and

turned her back to me, before demanding a gin martini with three olives. Then, with drink in hand she strode away.

"Who's that?" Ruth whispered. "A temperamental actress?"

"No. A temperamental ex-girlfriend. She was involved with Wade Lambert. You remember him?"

"No, never met him."

"He was the assistant director who visited Harmony ahead of the film crew to check out the place. I thought you were with me, but no loss on your part if you didn't meet him. He struck me as a snobbish sort. Unnecessarily rude. Even Kim told him off while showing him around to the likely sites they'd be shooting at. And if Kim did that to a client you know he's got to be bad. Sounds like Wade has a couple of people looking for him. I thought he'd be here tonight."

"So did I," Dennis said.

My shoulders slumped. Oh no. Not him again. "Aunt Ruth, meet the director of *Becoming Beverly*."

Dennis leaned in and put his finger softly up against my mouth. "Please don't say that. My daughter Alli is the official director. I'm her Sherpa, here to guide her up the mountain ahead. And who is this charming woman?"

"I'm Ruth Parker. So pleased to meet you, Mr. Turner."

Stu interjected himself saying, "And I'm Stuart Walters. Otherwise known as Kim's husband."

"Ah yes, I've heard about the lovely Kim. You are a lucky man. I am trying to keep relationships straight. You are Robert Parker's sister?"

Ruth nodded. "So, no relation to Beverly. But I am a fan of her work in *Times of Our Life*."

"That was a very popular soap opera. Bev made her fortune portraying Pauline Dubois," Dennis said.

Since I hadn't avoided him being next to me again, I might as well ask about Shayne and Dionne. "Are the actors playing my mother and father here tonight? We'd enjoy meeting them."

"I think they are both here. Shall I bring them over to meet you, Ruth?" Dennis suggested.

"I'd enjoy that," Ruth said. "If it's not too much bother."

"Nonsense, no bother at all. They will probably want to pick your brains about the characters they are portraying. Bev was so stunned by all that Alli uncovered about her biological father. Then came that visit here where the pieces fell in place, and she got to meet her mother's family. That overwhelmed her. I'm sure you were stunned as well. I'll try to find Shaye and Dionne."

"He seems nice," Ruth said. "It's exciting to have this

happening here in Harmony. But I must say, it brings back some difficult memories for me."

"I'm sure it does, Ruth. I didn't have those same memories." I couldn't catch myself from saying the next words. "Because you kept things from me."

Ruth flinched. I already regretted what I'd said.

"You were too young, Jackie." Ruth lowered her eyes. "It really was unnecessary that you be exposed to what happened."

"I've been a grown woman for a very long time, Aunt Ruth. I don't understand why, after all these years, I had to find out in such a public way."

"Your father couldn't bear to have you learn about your mother's betrayal of her marriage vows." Ruth's voice faltered before she continued. "I had to respect that, Jackie. I kept the vow I made to him."

"That you would never reveal it to me? It would just be swept under the rug?"

"It would have been the scandal of the decade here if word got out," Ruth said, her eyes imploring me for forgiveness.

Looking at this dear woman who had loved me as a mother and kept that secret for so long, my sense of betrayal lifted. What was the point? Who am I to judge decisions made decades ago?

"I'm sorry, Jackie."

Ruth felt small as I wrapped my arms around her. "I shouldn't have jumped on you like that. You were caught in the middle."

"Those times were hard. And not just for us. I always thought that Mary Bell knew her husband wasn't faithful. That Joanna wasn't his first dalliance. But to do it with a local woman and then the pregnancy. Mary was never the same afterward."

"You've been talking to Granny G, haven't you?"

"And to Eleanor. The Bell and the Harmony families ran in the same social circles. I heard they will film a scene at the mansion as well." Ruth squeezed my hands as her eyes looked past me and a soft smile rose to her lips. "Here comes the man playing Bob. He looks so much like your dad."

The glimmer in Ruth's eyes made me hesitate to look at the man who would portray my father. But with a deep breath I did. Middle-aged and fit, with a full head of dark brown hair. Comfortable stride. At ease in his own skin. Just like Dad.

"So, this is my character's sister?" Shayne said, taking Ruth's hand between his. "I've wanted to meet you. Did I remind you of your brother when I came up? I hope they are wonderful memories."

"Yes, very good memories," Ruth said with a catch in

her voice. "Shayne, this is my niece. Your daughter, so to speak. Jacqueline Parker."

The sound of breaking glass startled us all. It was Eleana. She'd stumbled against something. Her martini glass lay at her feet. The angry, bad-tempered person she was a few seconds ago now looked defeated. I was grateful to see Dennis and Alli come out of the crowd and guide Eleana outside, away from the attention she'd drawn to herself.

"She's having a rough day," Stu said.

Shayne nodded. "I don't know her, but I've heard she had a romantic breakup. Alli doesn't need these distractions. Now, I'd love to hear about your brother, Ms. Parker. May I ask you a few questions?"

I was glad to see Aunt Ruth welcome Shayne's questions. Since she was occupied, I decided to catch up with Alli. This was the first I'd seen of her tonight. She stood at the edge of the patio looking down toward the small dock below.

"Sending her back to the marina with Matt?" I asked as I stepped up next to Alli. She looked tired. Stressed out.

Down below Dennis was helping Eleana board the pontoon boat. Matt gave her his jacket for the chilly ride ahead. They backed out and motored away into the darkness.

"Will she get up to the B&B okay by herself?" I said.

"I almost don't care anymore. The boat ride should clear her head. She'll be fine. We're in a small town. What can happen?"

"I'm glad to see you made it here tonight," I said.

There was my usual smiling niece back again. She reached to give me a quick hug. "Me too, Aunt Jackie. I'm going to mingle and make my face seen. But I don't plan on staying long. It's been a tiring day."

"I can't even imagine," I said.

Dennis walked back up the stone steps. "Thanks for the idea about getting her on the boat going back to Harmony. There's another call coming in. I'm stepping out front where I can hear better. I'll be back shortly."

"He's always busy with calls and proposals and I don't know what all," Alli said. "But I'm so happy he made time to be here with me."

I stood looking across the river, hoping Matt would make it to the builders' award event.

CHAPTER FIVE

hen I tried to reach Scott the next morning to see how the award ceremony went, the call went to voicemail. Kirsten was here again today to monitor things inside Parker Photography as they readied it for filming. She was grateful for the extra hours because the studio was closed to customers, and she could work on her college assignments.

"How'd it go yesterday?" I asked. "Did you have to stay late?"

"Went okay. They told me that this was an easy setup. About six people came and painted walls, then hung up old portraits from the ones you guys had stored here. Said they were going over to Sutton's Antiques to help there next and that they will paint our place white again when they're done."

"That's the deal," I said. "Did they stay long?"

"No. But I stayed until shortly after nine."

"Wow. Why so late?"

"It was quiet so I could work on my term paper," Kirsten said. "I hope that was okay with you."

"Absolutely. I appreciate you locking up and keeping an eye on Libby for me."

"She's such a sweetie. I love her cuddling up at my feet while I work. I told her she needs to rest up for her big screen debut," Kirsten said. "Do you know the schedule for today?"

"No but I'm on my way to the Village Hall to pick it up. Catch you later!"

Outside the Village Hall there was a line of people waiting to see if they could get a walk-on role as an extra. Ever since word that the memoir *Becoming Beverly* would film in Harmony and that extras dressed in 50s and 60s fashion could show up on the day of filming, residents had been raiding their closets to piece together apparel from a bygone era. Some had even sewn their own dresses. Lucky for them that the large pattern companies had reissued patterns from those times.

All ages were welcome to apply. And by the looks of

it, many were here to do just that. They formed a long line of all shapes and sizes. A baby with a large bonnet sat in an old-style baby stroller pushed by a young couple. Behind them in the line was a stooped man in a red and black buffalo plaid shirt. Suspenders held up his well-worn wool pants. He hung on to the hand of a young child in blue bib overalls. I noticed Aunt Ruth chatting with a barrel-chested man fussing with his dark mustache. Next to her stood Betty and Dorothy.

"No Eunice or Harry or Elmer?" I asked.

"Nope. They didn't want to bother," Betty said. "I have a suspicion they plan on sneaking in on the filming to photo bomb it. I want to make this on my own merits as an actress. Back in the day I performed the role of Alice. The Alice."

"From Arlo Guthrie's song?" Dorothy said dryly.

"No silly. Alice in Wonderland."

"Was that fourth grade or fifth grade?"

"Dorothy don't pop her bubble," Ruth scolded. "I've never been in a production of any size. Are you going to get your costume today, Jackie?"

"I am. And I have to get a call sheet to see where I need to be and when."

"Hey, how do you rate?" Dorothy said. "We've been hoping Ruth's influence will get us a part. Maybe we should have been counting on you."

"I'd love to see myself on the big screen," Betty mused. "What a life achievement that would be."

"I bet you will all get in. I mean look at those outfits you have. Ruth, I remember that dress. You wore it often while working in the studio. And in one of those pockets, you always kept a handkerchief."

With a warm grin that twinkled up to her eyes, Ruth pulled an embroidered hankie out. I gave her a big hug and whispered, "I love you."

At just that moment Alli walked by with a leather tote bag full of papers. "Good morning, ladies! Hey Aunt Jackie, they're looking for you in wardrobe. First trailer back on the side street."

"I don't get my own dressing room?" I teased.

Alli laughed. "Ah… No! Remember this is a low budget film. Mom holds the purse strings, and she's keeping them tight. Oh Ruth, you should have told me you wanted to be an extra. I'll text the casting director right this minute to make sure you are in."

"Thanks, Alli. Could I impose and have my friends Dorothy and Betty added in also?"

"Of course. I'd be happy to. Your costumes are perfect. You'd be shoe-ins without my help. Gotta run. We're setting up on Oak Street. See you guys later."

The wardrobe trailer was busy. In the middle of it,

Kim held court atop a foot high platform. A woman adjusted the fit of her dress while they chatted.

"This is so fun. Just look around this place. And Jackie, wait until you see your outfit."

"Still now, Kim," the seamstress said, pulling a pin out of her mouth to speak. "I'm taking a tuck in this seam like you asked. Though I hope it doesn't break when you move. Seems a bit snug."

Kim rolled her eyes in my direction. "I appreciate your opinion and expertise, but it feels great. And Connie, the other way was just too frumpy and old looking."

"This is a shift dress style. It's not meant to be skintight. That's not the way women wore it. I might get in trouble for making these changes. They alter the authenticity of the garment."

"I can shift around in it just fine. Plus, I have influence here," Kim said. "You let me know if anyone gives you grief."

"Right. Sure. That's what they all say," Connie said with a chuckle. "There you go, my dear. Good luck with your scene."

"Thanks," Kim said as she stepped down. "I'm ready for my acting debut."

"Ms. Parker, if you'll come this way, I have your costume ready to try on. I think you'll look great in this shade of blue. It will be a stunning color against your complexion and gray hair."

I loved it! The waist-hugging coat with wide lapels fit me right off the hangar. White gloves and pearls were added along with a wide-brimmed hat with a shallow crown. Next came thick heeled pumps with peekaboo toes and a leather purse with a clasp top.

"I love the hat. Laura, our costume designer chose it. She's the best."

"I have memories of these styles from the dress shop my mother owned. She loved fashion. It was such a big part of her life."

"And yours too, I suppose. You have a terrific figure. Tall, long legged, slender. Were you ever a model?"

"No way, except for my mother's friends. She'd dress me up in an outfit so I could model for her friends who had daughters. I was not into it like she was. I took after my father who had a photography business. That was my profession, and I loved it as much as she loved hers."

"Say, are you Beverly's half-sister? I'm just putting that together now. My name is Connie. It's a pleasure to meet you, Jacqueline Parker."

"How do you know about that?"

"I read the memoir and Kim over there filled me in on the story not told in the book. The part of the story they're filming here." Connie stood back to take me in. "There. Perfect."

"Thanks, Connie. I just come back here after my scene is shot?"

"Yes, ma'am. Have fun!"

When Connie heard Kim asking me if I wanted to go up to see the filming on Oak Street, she said we shouldn't risk doing too much in our costumes.

"The call sheet schedule said the filming at Vogue on Main doesn't start for over four hours. That's too long to sit around," Kim pleaded with Connie. "If we are very, very careful, can we pretty please go there in these dresses?"

"Filming isn't always as glamorous as you might think," Connie said. "It's a lot of hurry up and wait. Like now, I'll bet there are people out there waiting for their fittings. This operation has been running catch as catch can." She opened the door to the outside, but no one was there. "That's strange. I hope they know where they are supposed to go. I mean, I have a list of costumes to fit today. Wonder where everyone is."

Kim's phone dinged. She gasped. "They've discovered a body at the Village Hall." She looked up at Connie. "It's your director."

"Oh my," Connie said.

"Not Alli," I cried.

"The text is from Stu and reads, *director dead.*"

"Kim, call Stuart and make sure you're understanding him right. I just saw Alli before I came here. She was walking up to Oak Street. This can't be true. Maybe Dennis? He's called the director too."

Her phone dinged again. Kim let out a relieved sigh and shook her head. "I'm so sorry to scare you like that, Jackie. Do you remember that man I was taking around town a while ago? The one who asked those awful rude questions?"

"Yes," I cried. "But what does he have to do with Alli?"

CHAPTER SIX

"Nothing." Kim looked perplexed. "She's fine."

My knees buckled at hearing Alli was okay.

"It's Wade. You met him at the diner. That's whose body they found! He called himself a director. But he is only an assistant director. Pretty nervy of him to lead me on like that."

I didn't hear the rest of Kim's rambling. I bolted out the door of the wardrobe trailer and headed toward the Village Hall, yanking the wide-brimmed hat off my head. Kim came running after me. Once I turned the corner onto Main Street, I saw Alli hurrying toward the Village Hall too.

"You've heard?" Alli cried. "Wade is dead. This can't be true."

Joyce, Patti Hunt's assistant, stood blocking the entrance to the Village Hall. When she saw Alli she moved aside to let her in.

"Aunt Jackie, please come with me. I could use your support."

Joyce waved me through.

"Hey! What about me?" Kim shouted. "My husband is in there somewhere. I need to get in to support him, too."

"Sorry, Kim. Patti told me to stop anyone from entering until she okays it," Joyce said.

Alli and I went down the stairs to the basement passing other staff who looked shell shocked. Patti saw us. Sadly shaking her head, she said, "I'm so sorry, Alli. We're not sure what happened yet. Our janitor found Wade this morning when he emptied the wastebaskets in the editing room."

Jeff stepped out of the editing room. "Good morning, ladies."

Alli pulled herself together. "I'm Allison Turner. Wade Lambert worked for me. Do you know what happened? Was it a heart attack?"

"I doubt it. More likely it was the bullet through his heart."

I grabbed Alli as she wobbled, her legs threatening to give out.

"I don't understand," she said, sinking into the chair I directed her to. "Who'd want to kill him? This just isn't possible."

"Jeff, do you have a time of death?" I asked.

"Well, well. Jacqueline Parker. Here we are again," Jeff said. "I suppose you'll tell me you don't want to be involved. How that was just a quick question."

I grinned. "You're right. I shouldn't have asked about the time of death. Except Alli is my niece and I'm here to support her."

Jeff nodded. "Ah, I see. As to your question, he died last night but we don't have a time yet. The medical examiner is still examining the body. Ms. Turner, do you know why the victim would have been working here long into the evening instead of at the Stone Mill where I understand the cast and crew gathered?"

"I knew he stayed late last night. He wanted to work with Marta on the film we'd shot in New York," Alli said in a shaky voice. "I hoped he would join us, but he wasn't a very social fellow."

"Patti, how can this space be accessed after the village offices close?"

"We gave Alli two keys to the front entry to the building. The door to our wing of offices is a separate key," Patti said. "Clubs and groups often use the gymnasium or this basement area in the evenings and on the weekends. Giving them a key to use was easier than locking up and such. And we have always placed trust in the people using it."

"Did the victim have one of those keys?" Jeff asked.

"I kept one and the other one I gave to Laura, our costume designer. She wanted to get the dressing rooms set up. I directed her to give it to Wade when she was done."

"Could you have Laura come by the police station today? I'd like to talk to her and pin down the last time she saw Mr. Lambert alive. And the Marta you mentioned too, please. Do you know of any employees who carry guns?"

Alli shuffled her feet and fidgeted with the edge of her chair.

"Alli, is something wrong?" Patti asked.

"I only know of one. Me."

Jeff nodded but didn't speak.

"I've carried one for my personal protection for years now."

"I understand. I'll need to see your gun as soon as possible."

"Of course, Chief. I'll retrieve it shortly, if that's okay. It's in my room at the B&B."

"If you're certain of that, I'm okay waiting to get it until later."

"Thank you Chief. Jackie, would you please go up to the filming on Oak Street? Dad took over for me when I was called away. Just let him know what's happening here," Alli said.

A tall, thin, gangly Ichabod Crane looking character walked out of the editing room. "Chief, I'm done. Can they pick up the body now?"

"Sure, Doc."

The doctor walked back into the scene of the crime.

"Our new doctor?" I asked. "I'll have to introduce myself. I didn't know they found a permanent replacement for Dawn."

"Oh sorry. I thought you would have already met," Patti said. "Peter Potter will be a good fit for Harmony. His wife Pamela is a teacher at the elementary school."

I stopped the snicker riding up my throat. Peter and Pamela Potter? Cute. "I'll go up to Oak Street to tell Dennis. Please call if there's anything else I can help you with here."

Two of Jeff's officers arrived in the basement just as we heard loud shouting coming from upstairs. It sounded like Joyce was having trouble blocking someone from entering. Next thing Eleana came charging down the stairs, screaming Wade's name.

CHAPTER SEVEN

"I need to take a break. Mind if I walk with you up to Oak Street?" Patti asked. "What do you make of all that? A murder in the Village Hall. Right down in our basement."

"Well, it is certainly shocking. I hope Jeff finds the murderer quickly. My sense is that this only involves the movie people. No one local would have done something like this," I said.

"Agreed. I can't fathom that a person would just shoot and kill someone like that. Will Wade's ghost haunt the Village Hall now?"

I almost burst out laughing but I could see she was dead serious. "Do you believe that sort of thing, Patti?"

"I do. I have a sense about ghosts and spirits."

To exaggerate my skepticism, I twisted my lips and pinched my eyebrows. It worked.

Patti fought back a grin in order to scold me. "Don't look at me like that. It's true. When I go tend to my vegetable garden at our old family farm, I feel my parents' spirits."

"Come on, Patti. That's different. Of course, we feel the presence of loved ones in places they inhabited. That's natural, isn't it?"

"You could say that, but not all people feel that. Like Charlie. He doesn't believe me. I know it. If I try to say something to him about it, his eyes glaze over. He tunes me out. Do you feel your parents anywhere?"

"Good question. I think about them often. I used to imagine what it would be like if they were still alive. There was so much I wanted to share with my dad when my photography career grew. Or with Mom when I'd get a new outfit. I knew she'd be happy to see me out of jeans. But I don't know that I feel their presence ever."

"See, it's not that common."

"Maybe you're more in tune? I think that's a possibility. You could have a sixth sense. But back to Wade. I doubt his spirit will hang around the basement," I said. "I don't remember you ever mentioning things like this about the others. Do you ever see Alan Morris' ghost at your farm?"

"Nope. But I wouldn't have expected to. Remember he didn't die there. Winford brought his body there to hide it."

"True. What about Luella at Eleanor's house? You've been back to that place."

"You must remember Eleanor told us that Harmony House has ghosts. So sure, they are there. But I can't say I've felt Luella's ghost. But then she didn't lay there all night like Wade did either. Oh, never mind, I know this all sounds way out there."

"No, it doesn't. I just guess I've never thought much about ghosts," I said. "Except for right now. I think I'm seeing my own ghost. Is that me coming out the front door of our old house?"

"That would be more of a time travel thing," Patti teased. "Because the girl you're seeing is the young actress, Bella Cameron. She's playing you."

My mind tried to grasp that this was happening. That a piece of my life would be on the big screen. The actress, Bella, was recreating a scene from my childhood. We watched her step out to the porch of my old home, the house I grew up in. She turned back to look inside the house, as if someone had called her. Then my mother stepped out and handed me a jacket. I mean Dionne Stockton handed Bella a jacket. Bella ran down to the sidewalk where the actor playing my father stood.

What was his name again? But before I could pull it up into my brain, I heard the word *cut* shouted. Everyone stopped as the cinematographer adjusted the cameras. He was a small, edgy man, with constrained movements. Focused. Pulling his reading glasses from atop his sandy hair to look through the camera lens.

"Should we talk to Dennis now?" Patti said.

"No, it looks like they are doing the scene again. Look. There's Kay. Let's go by her."

"Isn't this exciting? You missed the shot of the Judge leaving my place. They did some interior things earlier. I'm so glad the house will be in the movie. I can use it in my promotional materials!" Kay said. "And look, Rod handed me this signed photograph. I was hoping Grannie G would be here."

Dennis noticed me standing near Kay. He waved me over as he took off his headset. "Jackie, have you heard from Alli? She left in a hurry. What's going on? Wait. They're ready to redo the scene. Let me finish this one and then we can wrap up here."

He put the headset back on and redirected his focus. It was interesting to observe his professionalism as he consulted with Lewis and the cameraman before the filming began.

I watched myself come out of the house again, get the jacket from my mother, and run across the lawn to my dad waiting on the sidewalk. It seemed innocent enough. Where would this scene fit into the film?

"Okay everyone, that's a wrap. Lunch awaits. We'll set up at the Vogue shop next. Find out if Wade has the place ready for us," Dennis said to a young man hovering nearby.

"Yes, sir. Will do."

"Ah Dennis, that's what I'm here to tell you. We have some bad news. Wade Lambert is dead."

Dennis was shocked.

Patti joined us. "It's true. We found his body in the editing room and didn't want to announce it to everyone until we told you."

"Wade? Dead? That can't be. I mean how? What happened? Accident? His heart?"

"Murdered," Patti said. "It happened last night."

Dennis began shaking his head. "That's crazy. Poor Alli. Is that why she was called away? Is she alright? I have to get to her."

"She's with our Chief of Police right now," I said. "We'll walk back down with you."

As we left the set, I noticed the cinematographer's gaze following us. When he caught me watching him, he quickly averted his eyes. Had he overheard us?

CHAPTER EIGHT

Knowing Dennis would be there to comfort Alli, I was left wondering what the rest of the day would look like. I was still in my outfit from the fitting earlier.

"Do you think they'll continue filming today? Or should I get out of my costume?" I asked Patti.

"Let me go in and see if anyone has decided yet." Patti disappeared inside the building but quickly returned saying that Alli would be out shortly. While we waited, Patti told me that Beverly Turner would arrive this evening. "I've made up a basket of goodies for her room to welcome her back to Harmony. Would you go with me later to take it up to her? I expect she'll have heard this news and I would feel less awkward if you were along, since you know her."

"I'd love to go with you," I said.

"What a mess she's walking into," Patti said. "Oh look, here they come. Listen, we'll catch up later. I have a day job to take care of."

Alli came up and gave me a hug. "I'm so glad you waited here. It means a lot. But now I've got to get things rolling again."

Dennis followed Alli's lead by hugging me too. "She's a strong soldier and will push through this shock by getting back to work. The show must go on. Looks like you'll be delivering your lines this afternoon, Jackie. I'll be there to watch."

"I'm counting on you and Alli to direct my performance. I've done nothing close to this."

"I'm sure you'll handle it perfectly," Dennis said, giving me a peck on the cheek before he hurried to catch up with Alli.

"Looks like you're in with the in crowd."

"Scott! What a delightful surprise."

"Who was that guy?"

"Alli's father, Dennis Turner. The famous director."

"Ah, I see. Don't go all Hollywood on me, Jackie." Scott teased. "Want to take a hike with me on the bluff walk tonight? We could end up at my place for a glass of wine."

"Sorry, but I can't. I just promised I'd go with Patti to greet Beverly Turner. She'll be arriving tonight."

"Hmm, so see the wife later while her husband is flirting with you this afternoon?"

"Scott, he wasn't flirting. That's just his way. Besides, he's an ex-husband."

"Ex, huh? I understand he was at the Stone Mill last night."

Matt must have told Scott what he saw.

I reached up to touch Scott's face. "How did the awards ceremony go? Bet my handsome guy stole the show."

"It went great." Scott pulled back. "Wish you could have been there. Look, maybe we can get together once this circus leaves town. See you later, Jackie."

Now what was that attitude about? So what if I wasn't there for him last night and had already made plans for tonight so I couldn't take a walk? "Men," I muttered under my breath.

Main Street was blocked off for filming. Crew members milled about. Alli talked with Lewis the cine-matographer while cameras were rearranged at their direction. Aunt Ruth, Dorothy, and Betty sat on the bench in front of the studio with my sweet Libby resting at their feet, waiting to be part of the background for the next scene.

Kim approached me. "Who do you think killed him? I heard he was shot once. Bam. Hit the ground. Poor Jeff, to be thrown in the middle of a murder again. Are you ready, Jackie? I think we need to get over to the set. I'm so nervous. How do I look?"

Knowing Kim like I do I skipped her first two questions and answered number three. "You look like a clerk in a women's dress shop did in the 50s. Classy and smart."

Kim twirled in front of me. "I hope I don't steal the scene."

A crew member approached us. "You two know your lines, right?"

We both nodded.

"Please wait over there for further direction."

Kim and I joined cast members Dionne, Shayne and Bella...Mom, Dad, and me. Cameras and boom microphones were positioned while Alli explained the scene being filmed. Mom would leave Parker Photography and cross Main Street to her shop.

Filming began. Ruth, Betty, and Dorothy were given the cue to chat among themselves. Shayne, performing as my father, stood in the studio waving goodbye to Mom. Bella walked off as if headed to school, stopping to pet Libby and give her a treat! It would be interesting to see how this all looked when it was edited together for the movie and not isolated in these short snippets.

Dionne's elegant walk across Main Street is how I remembered Mom looking. The camera panned to follow her. A car drove by, and the man waved to Dad. Extras on the sidewalk greeted Dionne as she entered Vogue on Main. And *cut* was called.

Kim and I were told to go into the store and prepare for the next scene. They repositioned cameras and adjusted lights around us.

For the first scene Kim was filmed as the store clerk was saying good morning to Dionne aka Joanna. Then they filmed me coming in and Kim asking if she could help me. From yet another camera angle, I was filmed entering and glancing around while Kim repeated her lines.

Rod Jessup showed up dressed as Judge Bell. Why would he be here? I soon learned why as I watched his scene. He was waiting for his wife. He exchanged flirtatious looks with my mother, who stood to one side near the register. Could that have happened?

I was called to come back into the scene to say hello to Mary Bell, who smiled and nodded to me before I turned to greet Judge Bell.

I felt light-headed.

Get a grip, Jackie.

This isn't real.

They're taking artistic license, making things up. But could the beginnings of an affair have happened this way?

I watched as Kim rang up Mary Bell's purchase on an old-style cash register and then folded the garment in tissue before placing it in a box. Kim tied the package with a yellow ribbon and pulled out one of the stylish yellow and white striped shopping bags I remember seeing as a child. The scene ended there.

Next scene was of my mother talking with the Judge, telling him she was traveling to New York for the spring shows. Her ending lines, spoken as Mary walked up, expressed the hope that he would bring his lovely wife back in to check out the new styles when they arrived.

It could have happened this way. The truth of that hit me. The meetups could have been arranged this simply.

Cut.

"Jackie, you're supposed to be shopping. We'll reshoot the scene. Please watch where your eye focus goes. And get ready for your line when Kim approaches you. Clear?" Alli said.

I'd forgotten I was still in the view. The camera saw me among the dress racks beyond Dionne and Rod. Mom and the Judge. "Sorry. I'll do it right this time."

CHAPTER NINE

Beverly opened the door to her suite at The Hills Resort and greeted me with a cheek kiss-kiss. Patti stood back, juggling a large basket filled with all things local, as she retrieved her ringing phone from her purse. I took the basket away and stepped into the room while she remained in the hall to take the phone call.

Beverly fussed over the goodies for a minute then set the welcome basket down on a small credenza. "Thank you very much. What a lovely treat."

Her suite opened to a sitting area with windows looking out over the golf course. Nice digs.

"I'm hoping you'll stay for an extra day, and we can get to know each other a little better," I said. "Everyone in Harmony is pleased that a part of your life story will be filmed here."

I noted that Beverly looked exhausted irrespective of the dusting of blush on her cheeks. She didn't respond to my remark, instead walking to the small bar on a side wall and picking up a wine bottle. She lifted it and read the label.

"The resort was gracious to leave this wine for me. I believe I'll open it right now."

Patti came into the suite, closing the door behind her and I made introductions. I could tell she was a little star struck. I didn't blame her. My sister Beverly was a striking woman. Wearing a simple silk shirt, and slacks that hung perfectly from her slim hips, she moved with a natural ease. The soft floral scent of perfume trailed her as she served the wine.

"Sorry. But I had to take that call," Patti said. "This suite is gorgeous. I suppose you're used to living in a style like this."

Beverly smiled. "My life does come with some perks. But since I'm financing this film instead of starring in it, I'm footing the bill for this suite myself instead of being compensated with such luxury."

"It surprised me that Alli added Harmony into the film, as it wasn't part of your book," Patti said.

Beverly offered a toast. "To my daughter's choices.

May they be wiser than mine." After clinking glasses, she took a seat opposite us.

"But it is part of your life story," I said. "I heard how persistent Alli was in finding your birth parents so I would suppose she was excited to bring the film crew here."

Beverly turned away to fluff the pillow next to her. "That she was."

"Will you sneak into the filming at some point? So movie goers and your fans can look for you?" Patti asked.

"I hadn't thought about that. I wouldn't want to steal any thunder from my daughter's efforts."

"Beverly, may I suggest a place where you won't be easily recognized?" I said. "I know they are filming at our local beauty shop tomorrow. Might be perfect to appear there. You could sit under a hair dryer."

"And without makeup. You are so stunning you don't need it," Patti said. "Or get all dolled up for tomorrow night at the Harmony mansion."

"What are they filming there for?" Beverly asked.

"Ruth suggested the Harmony House as a place for the Judge and Joanna's paths to have crossed. High society and all," I said. "But I don't think my parents were part of that circle."

"Ruth must have thought so," Beverly said.

"We filmed at Vogue dress shop today and the scene had Joanna and the Judge talking in a flirtatious way while his wife shopped. Wouldn't that have been enough since no one knows how the affair was handled?" I sounded defensive even to my own ears. How did the two of them pull it off? How did it start? Don't even go down that road again, Jackie. Move on.

"I can see it makes you uncomfortable," Beverly said. "Me as well. How did our mother manage the affair? Leaves one wondering. This is a small town. She and her paramour were both well known in the community."

Beverly downed her entire glass of wine and stood up. "Alli spoke of letters and paperwork found in the old files left at the Bell house. She researched and found that Josiah Bell traveled to New York and Los Angeles on dates that coincided with times they held the apparel markets. She surmised that was when they met up."

Wanting to shift the conversation to something else I said, "Have you been to some of the other sites where filming was done?"

"Before I polish this bottle off, did either of you want more wine? I'm thirsty. Travel does that to me."

Without waiting for an answer, Beverly poured herself another glass of wine and continued speaking. "Yes, I have. Los Angeles, of course, because I live there now. That is where the biggest hunk of the filming will be from. Showing my life as a movie actress, meeting my husband, having a baby."

Beverly walked to the window and looked up at the night sky. "Not to the New York film set though. The city tires me. It was a hard time. I learned I'd been adopted and left my Florida home in anger. I struggled to get work in the theater district. A tough existence and few good memories."

"What about Florida?" I asked. "Did you revisit your old neighborhood?"

"I did. Alli convinced the family living in my old home to let us take it back to the past for a few days. That was very emotional for me. But in a good way. Looking back, I've grown to realize I had a wonderful childhood," Beverly said with a wistful tone. "But this part of it...I don't know. I almost didn't come."

"Well, I'm happy to see you again. I'll bet Alli is glad you are here."

"One would hope. I'm aware that my ex Dennis is unhappy I showed up. We call our divorce amicable. That's Hollywood speak for don't ask. We both are driven people. When I learned he was going to be working on the set with Alli in a sort of apprentice relationship, I was not pleased about it."

"But isn't he a renowned director? And this is Alli's first directing position, right?" Patti asked. "Sounds like a good bonding moment for them over a shared interest."

"Alli tried acting after my begging her not to. This business can eat you alive. She found that acting wasn't her thing. Then her goal changed to getting behind the camera as a director. Funny how that worked out, now I'm paying my ex to be with our daughter," Beverly said.

"Sounds kind of like my relationship with my father and mother. I loved trailing after Dad and his sister Ruth when they ran the photography studio. The picture taking. Developing. Lighting. Angles That's what made this little kid smile. All of it. But my mother's dress shop? Nope! Not for me."

Beverly's eyes registered hurt even as a small smile rose on her lips. "Yes, we can't know how parenting will affect our children."

"You are lucky to have a daughter," Patti said.

"Yes, I am. But she puts my nerves on edge occasionally. If you'll excuse me. It's been a long day."

"Of course," Patti said. "Thank you for letting us share some time with you."

"And thank you for the welcome basket. Forgive me for my silly talk. I'm exhausted. Perhaps we'll see each other tomorrow."

"Do you have a car here? Or will you need a ride into town?" I asked.

"Alli will call with arrangements. But thank you," Beverly said, holding the door open. "Good night."

"Oh, one more thing Beverly. I don't mean to make your day worse, but did you hear…"

"About the murder. Yes. I did. Too bad. I hope your police chief will handle it locally. I wouldn't want the reporters to rain down on Harmony. Best if we can keep it quiet."

"Did you know Wade?" I asked.

"I knew him. He had good instincts about the movie business. But friends warned me he was a very ambitious person. Hollywood is filled with that type."

As the hotel door closed behind us, Patti whispered, "She seemed a little standoffish, don't you think?"

"In a way. But she was tired." I tried to shrug off my let down feeling. We hadn't even exchanged hugs. Beverly had a lot more invested in this visit back to Harmony than I realized. This time her daughter and ex-husband were both here. I hoped there wasn't more trouble brewing between them.

CHAPTER TEN

"That call earlier was from Mandy," Patti said as we walked away. "She asked if I'd like to come over to the Village Hall and see the editing end of filmmaking. Dave the Drone Dude is there too. They have hired him to do film footage both for the movie and for a promotional trailer."

"Is it okay if I take a peek too?"

"I'm sure it will be fine. You've met Beverly before. Don't you think there was more to her mood than being tired?"

I shrugged. "Like she said, this is hard for both of us. I had my parents to myself my entire life. You heard her say she had a wonderful life in Florida, but then how hard it must have been to learn about being adopted. She's told me she reconciled with her parents later on in life and changed her name to Beverly to honor her adoptive mother."

"But why the bad vibes about coming to Harmony again?"

"When I first met her, she said she'd had no burning desire to find her biological parents. But then Alli dug around and kept at it."

"You never told me about that night at the Stone Mill when you met Beverly, your half-sister," Patti said.

"It was a shock. Plain and simple. It started back when I was curious about Mary Bell. I walked the trail named after her and I met Granny G, who cleaned at the Bell mansion. She spoke of the sad time in the Bells' life. I wanted to know more. Eleanor Harmony was the one who got Aunt Ruth to tell me the story of my mother having given birth to a little girl and putting her baby up for adoption in Florida."

"Oh my, I would have liked to be a fly on the wall for that reveal. So, Ruth knew, but kept it a secret all those years?" Patti asked.

"She did. Times were different. Fast forward to Ruth and her Shady Pines gang, along with Rocco Montalvo, doing research to locate the child. That night at the Stone Mill was a serendipitous moment. Kay was there with Alli and Beverly to surprise Aunt Ruth. Ruth was a super fan of Beverly's acting in the soap opera. Alli was explaining her journey to find her mother's birth family here in Harmony, but she only knew about Josiah Bell being the father. She was…"

"Hold on, Jackie. How did Alli know all that?"

"She was curious…"

"Like her aunt. Sorry for interrupting. Go on."

"My curiosity has gotten me into some interesting situations. Alli's curiosity led her to letters from Josiah in papers her grandparents had boxed up and never shared with their daughter. Even after their deaths, Beverly didn't open the boxes. Alli discovered that the birth father had found out who adopted his daughter, which he probably accomplished because he was in the legal field. I was at the Stone Mill that night, and so was Rocco. Come to find out, Rocco had been sent a photograph from a New York theater district museum curator. It contained a photo of Caroline Smith, in other words, Beverly Turner before she changed her name. He took it to Ruth's table to show her what he'd found. Ruth showed Alli and Beverly the photograph. Of course, Beverly recognized herself in it, and Alli convinced her to admit it. From there the pieces tumbled into place."

"Wow," Patti said. "What a blessing that special night happened."

"Hi Mom," Matt said, as we walked into the screening room.

"I didn't know you would be here too," Patti said, giving her son a hug.

"Dave invited me over to show me his appreciation for helping him set up his website," Matt said, with a slap on his friend's back. "And he promised Mandy and me a beer as soon as we're done here."

"The film editor, Marta, asked me to stop by so she could show me her ideas for my drone video," Dave said. "Pretty cool stuff. I'll film a current flyover scene and then they'll use photos from the past to do a swirl or fade out back to those black and white photos. Or something like that, right Marta?"

Marta laughed. "Pretty close. Nice to meet you, Matt's mom."

Alli walked into the room with a distracted expression on her face but welcomed me warmly when she realized I was there.

"What are you all doing here? Is this where the party is?" Alli pointed to the chalk markings on the floor. "Sorry, I should get those cleaned up."

"I wanted to get back to work as soon as the Chief of Police cleared the scene," Marta said. "I'm glad you stopped by. I have some ideas Wade, God rest his soul, and I had been talking about. Now I want to run them by you."

"Sure Marta, I'm glad you're taking that on. I trust your judgment. With Wade gone I'll have to lean on you and Lewis even more. But right now I have to go up to The Hills. Mom just got into town. I don't know if she's learned about Wade's death yet."

"Patti and I just left her. We took a welcome basket to her. She knows about him," I said.

"Thanks for the heads up. She was the one who initially suggested Wade as director of the movie. I think she wanted me to act in it. But when I said I wanted to direct it instead, she agreed with one condition, that Wade stay on as assistant director. He was not pleased with that demotion."

"We're all here for you, Alli. We want this movie to be a great success," Marta said. "Rumor was your mother wasn't that happy about coming here to Harmony."

Alli nodded. "It's no big secret that Mom hated putting in this part of her story. She agreed to filming here but holds veto power on what makes the final cut."

"Why do you think that is?" I asked.

"I don't know, Jackie. It's so irritating to me. I worked hard to find her birth parents. I thought she'd like that. She makes me so mad sometimes. Why can't she just be happy about it? It was long ago. And now she has a family here. Sorry, everyone. My nerves are on edge."

"Understandable," Marta said. "There are a few other things I want to talk to you about, but they can wait. Strength, lady! You've got it. Remember it's your movie!"

Alli laughed. "Yeah right. Have you ever worked with my mother? I'll make time tomorrow, Marta. Is Lewis okay on his end? He mentioned something he was unhappy about."

"I think I know what he means. Either the camera operator didn't get the lighting right, or some sort of filter or effect was added afterward. I'll check on the scene he mentioned tonight while I'm here."

With a small droop to her shoulders Alli left the room. I felt bad for her. Instead of looking forward to her mother being here, she was expecting a confrontational situation.

Alli peeked back in to ask, "Have you seen Eleana today? She was so shaken up this morning."

"I saw her walking in the park near the marina earlier tonight," Mandy said. "She seemed okay. But I didn't talk to her."

"Would you like me to call her?" Marta asked.

"No. I'll check with Dad."

We all watched as Dave and Marta tightened up their ideas. It was fascinating to see our own Dave the

Drone Dude collaborating with a professional film editor.

When they finished, Matt invited us all to join them for a beer. Patti and I declined.

"Tempting as it is, I'll have to pass too. I want to stay here and look at that messed up film," Marta said.

As soon as I got home, Libby greeted me. "Hey girl. I've been neglecting you, haven't I? And there's someone else feeling just like you."

I tried Scott's cell phone, but it went to voice mail again.

CHAPTER ELEVEN

It took Libby awhile to get me up and out of bed the next morning. But I knew what would happen if I didn't let her out soon. So began the day. I checked my phone, but no message back from Scott. I vowed to make it up to him today.

Today was Todd's turn to be running things here at the studio. With the discovery of the body creating a filming delay yesterday, the crew would be inside my studio for a couple of more scenes. My business reopening would be delayed.

"Will Alli be able to manage without Wade's help?" Todd asked me as soon as I came in.

"Are you interested in my niece?"

Todd blushed. "As a friend. I appreciate her focus on

her goals. She's driven. I'm making plans to visit her in Los Angeles."

"Really? So, you'll be asking for time off?"

"I hoped to do an in-depth interview while she's here, but she's super busy, especially now with the thing yesterday. I may have suggested I fly out and conduct the interview there. And she may have agreed," Todd said with a grin. "So yes, some days off are requested."

The crews were gathering outside on Main Street. Today my studio, the Cut-n-Curl, and Dolly's Diner would be used as settings. I don't know how they planned on getting all that done in one day, but not my problem.

If none of my scenes had to be reshot, I think my days of being an actress were over. Today I would enjoy watching the process.

My phone rang. It was Aunt Ruth wanting to know if I had any more information about the murder.

Another call came in from Stuart Walters to see if I could provide more details.

What was I?

Information Central?

No, but I was the person everyone seemed to think about when a mysterious death happened. And I guess I couldn't blame them. Somehow, I was roped into several murder investigations since I returned to live in Harmony. But no way I'd have a connection to this one.

"See you later, Todd," I said, as my phone rang yet again.

My body deflated when Jeff Mathis' number showed up on my caller ID. The temptation not to answer was fleeting. In a town this small he'd find me in short order. With fingers crossed he wasn't calling to discuss Wade's murder, I answered the call. "Morning Chief. How's your day going?"

"Could be better. And you?"

I knew his reason for calling wasn't to find out how I was, but I'd play along. "Great. Going to relax today and watch my niece in action. Maybe I'll see you around. Take care now. Bye."

"Wait, Jackie! Don't hang up. I need your help."

"Do you need my baked pasta recipe to make for Kay and wow her?"

"Hilarious. No. I would like you to do me a favor. You're close to the movie people. Alli's your niece. Beverly is your half-sister. I know you spent time with Dennis at the Stone Mill party."

"Oh no you don't, Jeff! The guy's a flirt and he spent time with lots of people that night. Beverly just got in late last night, so she won't know anything. Yes, Alli is my niece, but I've barely gotten to speak with her since they all arrived. You know who's close? Who might get you some worthwhile information? Patti at the Village Hall. She's practically tripping over them. They are set up there on her turf. Patti's unobtrusive. Or Mandy. There you go. She's shooting photos as the unit photographer. She has an excuse to be in all sorts of places around them too. Or of course Kim. She worked with Alli and Wade on the leasing and she loves to help and finds out things no one else could. All good choices. Much better than me."

"I take that as a no?"

"A NO in all caps."

"I've talked to them already. Please don't be hurt that I didn't call you first. I need eyes and ears on the ground and I'm reaching out to anyone I can think of."

"If I hear anything I'll let you know. Okay. Bye now."

"No, wait! You aren't just anyone. You are special, Jackie."

"Sweet talker, aren't you? Don't toy with me. Why am I so special?"

"Your curiosity and intuitive powers are exceptional."

Jeff's voice seemed to have an echo. "Where are you, Jeff? I'm getting feedback."

The tap on my shoulder made me jump out of my skin.

Jeff clicked his phone off with a smile. "I could see you from my office and by all the avoidance tactics you were offering, I knew I had to come over and talk with you face to face. Help me please?" He held his hands in prayer position, with a pleading expression on his face.

I didn't know whether to smack him or laugh at his hangdog look. "Oh, all right. I told you already I'd listen for anything that might be a clue. What else can I do? Have you talked with the crew members? That seems your best chance at finding out who besides Alli had a gun."

"I have done that." Jeff's eyebrows rose questioningly. "But what if it's not someone in the crew?"

"You can't be serious. No one local would have a reason to shoot Wade Lambert."

"True, but there is someone I have in mind who is not local and who is not part of the crew," Jeff said. "I was hoping you might help me out by talking with her. Maybe offer to buy Eleana a drink. Commiserate with her losing her boyfriend. Girl stuff like that."

"Eleana? You think she did this? Then do a formal interview, Jeff. I only met the woman briefly at the Stone Mill."

"Did you know she was involved with Wade?" Jeff asked.

"Yes. We all do after her drama at the Village Hall yesterday."

"My understanding is that Wade asked Dennis or Alli to hire her as some sort of assistant."

"She was planning on staying on as Dennis's assistant. In fact, she was acting in that capacity at the Stone Mill party."

"See, there you go. You never know what might be good information!"

"Which you could have learned by interviewing her, Jeff." I waved my finger in his face.

He continued without losing a beat. "Now that Wade's dead she's shook up. Driftless in the Driftless, you might say."

I groaned.

"She's claiming they were engaged. I'm checking up on that. The producer of this movie wants to keep things quiet, so the crew is clamming up."

"The producer is Beverly Turner, Alli's mother, which I'm sure you know. She is fronting the money and I don't blame her for wanting things to settle down."

I tried to remember what she'd said last night. She knew about Wade's death but didn't want to talk about it. Last thing Alli needs is to have a murder linked to her directorial debut. If talking to Eleana helps keep things quiet for Alli, I'll do it. I'd do anything I could to help her.

"Look Jeff, for Beverly and Alli's sakes I'll see if Eleana will chat with me. She hasn't left town, has she?"

"No. She's booked in at Kay's place. She moved out of the room she was going to share with Wade after a big blowup the night they got here. Kay filled me in on that. But I suppose you already knew that?"

I didn't bother to answer him because Patti walked up to us and said, "Jackie, I was looking for you. Ruth and Dorothy appear in the Cut-n-Curl segments. Come on, let's head over there and watch. Here comes Beverly! And in a 50s costume. Maybe she let Alli know she wanted to be part of the scene."

"We'll talk later," I told Jeff as I turned to walk away.

He touched my elbow to stop me. "I appreciate anything at all. Oh, and Jackie, find out if Alli was telling the truth about her gun being stolen, would you? She might confide in you. Her quick remark about it seemed a little weak."

"What? When did you find that out?"

"Last night. She was supposed to turn it over to me but now claims it's missing from her room."

He returned my puzzled look with a palms up, what-can-I-say gesture. "So, I'm left without a murder weapon. From what I've learned no one else carried one. Maybe Alli will confide in you?"

"Jeff, I will not try to trick her. Please don't ask me to do that. I have to go now." And I turned to leave before he asked one more thing of me.

Ruth and Dorothy, pink plastic capes draped over their clothing, were being taken inside the beauty salon. Where was Val? She should be here to see this. Then I spied her being positioned under one of the old-fashioned hair dryers. She was going to be a customer in her own salon. How fun!

Beverly walked over to thank us for the suggestion. "I'm taking on a few lines too. You had a good idea last night. Sorry I was so out of it. Maybe we can all get together before I leave?"

She seemed refreshed after a night's rest.

"Of course. I'd enjoy that," I said.

Kim joined us too and elbowed me while smiling at Beverly.

"Beverly, have you met Kim Walters? She's the realtor who made all the arrangements for leasing sites here in Harmony."

"I'm so sorry about Mr. Lambert. He was such a dear man to work with. Please accept my deepest condolences," Kim said.

I almost choked. How death changes things. Kim was practically cussing at him the last time he was in town.

Beverly looked uncertain. "You'll have to excuse me. Alli will call action soon."

"Well, I got that hint big and loud," Kim said. "What did I ever do to her?"

"I wouldn't take it personally Kim," I said, even though I didn't know how else she could take it. That had been an abrupt dismissal of Kim.

Patti offered a suggestion. "I was watching her expression and her face hardened when you mentioned Wade. Maybe that has something to do with it?"

"And here I was trying to speak well of her employee. Geez. The guy was a rude snob. You remember, don't you, Jackie. That day in the diner. He asked that awful question and I snapped."

"Maybe she didn't care for him either?" Patti said. "Oh look. They're filming your mother walking into the salon. I wonder what this scene is about."

The answer came from Dennis. "They are going to be showing how Joanna was part of a small town, but just felt a bit above it all."

Kim nudged me again. She wanted another introduction. But Dennis did it on his own.

"And you are the lovely Mrs. Walters. I noted you

yesterday when you were in the Vogue dress shop scenes."

Kim did a little shoulder straightening and neck stretching, before slipping on her empathetic face. "Awful about Mr. Lambert, isn't it? I'm so sorry you lost an associate."

Kim licked her lips and adjusted her collar, turning it up just right to frame her face. "I loved that movie you directed, *Westward Bound.*"

"*Bound for the West,*" Dennis corrected her. "That's kind of you to say. It was one of my favorites too."

"I'm sorry we didn't get introduced at the Stone Mill party."

Dennis leaned in close to Kim. "I can't believe that either. Had I noticed you, I would have introduced myself."

Kim giggled. "I worked with Mr. Lambert on securing properties for the filming here. When I expressed my condolences to your wife...oops sorry, your ex-wife, she abruptly left without answering a question I'd asked. Did your wife dislike Wade?"

"I believe they've had a falling out. I'm helping Alli pick up the slack since he's gone. Good thing most of the filming is complete." Dennis looked toward the salon door where Beverly was getting direction from Alli. "But I'm surprised she was rude. You must have misunderstood her reaction, Maybe she needed to get in position for the shot. Alli mentioned to me that Bev wanted to appear in the film and decided this scene would work."

"We suggested that to her last night," Patti said. "I'm glad she is doing it. It'll be fun to see her on the big screen again."

Dennis was still staring. "Yes, she is a consummate actress."

CHAPTER TWELVE

We watched the filming from a distance. The salon space was so small I couldn't see much so I decided I might as well make some sort of attempt to talk to Eleana. But where was she?

When Patti said she was returning to the Village Hall, I went with her. At least I could show Jeff I made an attempt to talk to Eleana.

With the surprise addition of an evening ball scene at the Harmony mansion, the wardrobe staff had been tasked with acquiring appropriate evening wear. I knew they would find exquisite gowns and high style menswear from the 50s in the Harmony family clothing collection. It held an astounding amount of preserved apparel. Last year the Historical Society catalogued the garments, and I photographed them to create a coffee-table book.

Hannah Sutton knew of an antique clothing store in Madison. She convinced the owner to open early so she and Connie could check what they had. They were just arriving back with the garments they'd purchased there.

"Wow. You scored a good number of gowns and men's suits. That should be quite a soiree," Patti said to Hannah.

"It was fun to help. You know how I love antiques. Even clothes! Do you know what the scene is going to be about? We heard it will be a scene where the Judge and Joanna have a dance together and sparks fly. Do you think that might have happened?"

Again, the uncomfortable feelings I'd had yesterday in the dress shop scene came back to me. I couldn't keep my voice from cracking but I managed to answer. "No one really knows. But Eleanor Harmony said that her family threw many big events, and it could very well have occurred."

Things were quiet in the basement. I saw Jeff in the room where the body was found, and I almost slipped by him unseen.

Almost.

"Jackie! Were you trying to sneak by me?"

"Yes, I was. You're one clever detective. I have

nothing to share with you yet. I haven't seen Eleana and Alli has been busy all day."

Someone overheard us because a voice called out that Eleana had gone down to the marina to chill out. I yelled a thanks back. Eleana is spending a lot of time at the marina, was my immediate thought.

I pulled Jeff into the janitor's closet and shut the door. I didn't want big ears to hear us.

"What am I supposed to say to her? I can't just go like, hey girlfriend, what's up. I'm not that way."

"You will figure something out. Scott keeps his pontoon at the marina. Make like you had to do something on the boat. Or see if Rocco's on his boat. You're good at that sort of thing."

Hmm, Scott hadn't returned my call yet. Maybe going to the marina wasn't such a bad idea after all. I doubted he'd be there, but I could check.

"Okay, I'll walk down to the river. But don't hold your breath."

"Question for you," Jeff said, scratching his head. "We found the shell casing. It's a 9mm. The size of ammunition used in guns like Alli's."

Jeff pulled it out of his pocket and tossed it in the air. "Maybe someone interrupted the action, and the gunman fled. By evidence at the scene and the autopsy results, it appears Wade was walking toward the gunman. Maybe he reacted to having a gun pointed at him and he grabbed for it. We also found this note in the garbage."

Jeff handed it to me. It read *Can you meet tonight? Text me a time.*

"I've not revealed this to anyone yet. Please keep it that way, Jackie. I trust you."

Patti knocked on the door and opened it. "What are you two doing in there?"

Jeff put his arm around my shoulder. "I'm trying to convince Jackie to help me out with something."

Patti laughed. "I hope it's not something that would upset Scott. Joyce said he was looking for you earlier, Jackie. Something about taking a pontoon ride this afternoon. It's going to be unseasonably warm. It would be a terrific day for it."

Now visiting the marina sounded perfect. "I was just headed that way. I'll be in touch, Jeff."

As I approached the marina, only a short walk away from the village square, I saw Scott's pontoon still in his slip. Good. He'd hadn't left yet.

I looked around for Eleana but didn't see her. Maybe she'd taken a walk on the Mary-Go-Round trail that encircled the village. From what I understood, Mary Bell handled her heartache over her husband's dalliances by walking. Her efforts to create a walking path were appreciated and continued after her death. Now the trail linked to the Harmony Museum Nature Center, the Hills Resort, and the Driftless Golf Course.

I'm not sure why Scott would be on his pontoon this morning, but the message he left with Joyce might have been an olive branch to me. And I owed him one too. I approached the pontoon, eager to clear the air between us. But no one was on it. Had I missed him?

Disappointed, I turned to leave. Then I saw them. Scott and Eleana were approaching from the marina store with a bait bucket, bottles of water, and what looked like a lunch bag. I'd interrupted something.

"Good morning, Scott. Joyce said you were looking for me."

"Hey, Jackie. I did. Decided I deserved time off to enjoy this beautiful spring day. Then I found this young lady looking like she could use a distraction. I asked her to help me carry some things to the boat."

"How nice. Why didn't you return my calls, Scott?" I sounded churlish even to my own ears.

Scott noticed. "Yeah, sorry about that. Would you like to go fishing with us?"

Us? She is all broken up about Wade's death and now is out and about to go fishing with a man old enough to be her father. I tried telling myself I might be reading this wrong. Scott's a nice guy. He just saw someone hurting and is trying to help.

"Did you know Eleana grew up in Minnesota? And loves fishing?" Scott said.

"Oh. Midwestern girl? Are you feeling better, Eleana? Yesterday you were extremely upset. Screaming and sobbing over your boyfriend."

Scott shot Eleana a puzzled look. "I thought you said he was your fiancé."

"He was. But then we had a terrible falling out. That reaction yesterday was from the depths of my heart. No matter how I felt, he didn't deserve to die." A small sob escaped her lips. She took a deep breath before continuing. "It just poured out. I'm still struggling with it all and Scott saw that. He offered me a reprieve."

"Anyone would have done the same thing," Scott said.

"Are you planning to stay in town? I understand Dennis offered you a temporary job as his assistant. Or are you planning to return to LA now that you're alone?"

Eleana let out a hard sigh and closed her eyes. "Alone. Yes, I'm alone. I can't believe he's gone. Who would do such a thing?"

I was just getting wound up. "That's what the police are trying to figure out, Eleana. Do you know of anyone who would have wanted to see him dead, or anyone in the crew who is carrying a gun?"

Scott shot me a what-are-you-doing look while Eleana wiped her dry eyes.

"Yes, I do. Alli Turner has one. Your niece. Alli hated it when Beverly first hired Wade. Alli wanted to prove herself. She wanted to be the director and pick her own team. Of course, with lots of help from mommy and daddy. Wade made his own way up in the industry. And now he was upset that some snot-nosed, spoiled brat was making trouble for him."

"Her gun is missing," I said.

"Oh yeah, sure it is! Hidden is more likely. Can we go out now, Scott? I could use that morning on the water you suggested."

Stunned by the words just spoken, Scott took a step backward before saying, "Ah, yeah, sure. You are coming along, Jackie?"

I tried to read his tone. Did he want me to say yes, or no? Give me a sign, Scott. It didn't come. "Thanks Scott, but I think I'll let you two go alone."

"Your choice. Maybe we can catch up later?"

"Not tonight. I'm going to the filming at the Harmony House," I said before even thinking. I didn't have to go there. But I wanted to show him that after not calling me and then giving me a weak offer of a maybe date, I had things to do.

I left, walking away with a sense of urgency to get out of their sight. But where to go? Luckily, I ended up on Main Street where the filming was going at the Parker Photography Studio.

Alli consulted with the cinematographer Lewis, while Dennis stood off to one side. The scene involved my mother, father, and me.

My vision tunneled. I saw myself back then. Wanting to stay to work with Dad. Mom's disappointment. Her aloneness while Dad and I were together. They were going in two different directions. Should I have tried harder with Mom? Liked and appreciated her career? Her specialness?

Were Scott and I going in two different directions now too?

CHAPTER THIRTEEN

The Harmony mansion and grounds were lit up and would provide a glistening crown on the hilltop for drone video being filmed tonight.

When Eleanor Harmony remarried, for the fourth time, she downsized by returning to her family's first home near their lumber mill business. During that process, she donated the family mansion and much of the surrounding acreage to a not-for-profit museum and nature center for the community. Residents who were proud of their village and their heritage welcomed the move. Situated atop one of Harmony's hills, overlooking Lake Harmony that the Wisconsin river had formed, the site was perfect for tourists and locals alike. School groups loved visiting the museum and the nature center. The grounds, set up to handle large events, provided additional income.

The last evening gala I'd attended here was a fundraiser during which Kim Walters, looking stunning in a red figure-hugging gown, took a tumble down the grand front staircase. And then Luella Hagge's body, in an identical red gown, was found in one of the upstairs rooms. Certainly, put a damper on that evening.

Alli and the film crew worked on setting up outside shots of guests arriving. Because of the last-minute decision to include this scene, there was only one antique luxury car available to bring arriving guests. They relocated the cameras to show the couples walking on the flagstone sidewalk to the large porch.

Kim and I were part of a gathering audience directed to remain back until this part of the filming was complete. I was proud of my niece in her role as director. Dennis stood behind her with arms crossed, observing what she was doing. His nodding head showed his agreement with her decisions. Lewis Berry kept a watchful eye on the lighting and camera angles. I had heard that all the crew respected him and knew that the production was lucky to have him onboard.

Kim stepped up beside me. "Hey, Jackie. Quite a night for Harmony. This feels like the night of the fundraiser. All the lights in the gardens and on the porch."

"I'll never forget that night," I said.

"Ah, my red dress. It was a stunner. I haven't had an event to wear it to since then. Maybe we should do a gala here every couple of years. I love to get dressed up."

"It survived your fall down the stairs?"

"It did. And I did too, thank goodness. What a tumble I took. Learned my lesson on that one."

"What lesson was that?"

"Stay away from the top of stairs when the lights go out!" Kim laughed. "I still think the culprit thought he was pushing Luella down but got me instead."

Kim adjusted her lavender crop jacket before winking at me. "You know how I've loved being part of your crime solving life. If I was shoved, which could be true, you know, it lends a more mysterious air to my involvement."

I almost corrected Kim about my life involving crime solving, but I knew it was pointless. Instead, I used the opening to find something out.

"Interesting, Kim. I agree you have been instrumental in helping the Chief solve some recent murder cases."

"Why, I appreciate that, Jackie!" With a conspiratorial

lean toward me, Kim whispered, "I heard something you might be interested in. I understand Jeff has a note from someone asking Wade to meet them that night."

I was shocked. "How did you know that?"

"So, it's true. Sorry, didn't mean to trick you, but I wanted to confirm it." Her eyes widened, and she nodded her head toward the filming. "Ooh look, it's Eleanor! Is she playing her own mother? Too funny, yet so perfect."

I watched as Eleanor Harmony, dressed in one of her mother's gowns from the museum collection, greeted the arriving guests, which included my Aunt Ruth. Then I saw Rod as Judge Josiah Bell and the actress playing his wife step up into the glow of the entryway. This whisked me away to another time. Time warped back to what it had been like over fifty years ago. But my breath stopped when the next couple to step up were my parents.

"Jackie, you okay?" Kim asked, as I reached for her arm.

"Aren't they a stunning couple?" I couldn't take my eyes off them.

"The Judge? Yes, he is one handsome dude. Did you see him in *You Will Love Again?* Stuart even has a man crush on him, I think."

"No, I meant the actor and actress playing my parents," I murmured. My eyes remained glued to the scene unfolding. The Judge turned aside, allowing my mother to pass, and extended his hand to shake my father's.

"Dionne is beautiful too. Just like the photos of your mother I've seen. Both very striking women. I loved working with her in the scene at the shop yesterday. I think I delivered my lines exquisitely. And the cameraman assured… Oh look, here comes Alli!"

"Would you two like to come inside and watch the filming? Mom is going to be here tonight too and wants to see the interior shots. I figure as producer she gets some special treatment," Alli said with a light-hearted laugh.

"We'd love to! Wouldn't we, Jackie," Kim said with excitement.

"Okay, follow me. We've got a viewing area on the balcony tucked away where you should be able to see quite a bit."

Kim and I looked at each other and laughed. "There's a story about that balcony, but I'll save it for later," I said.

"This place is amazing. I'm so glad Ruth suggested it. We'll be moving you to watch the dance sequence in the sunroom. That should be pretty cool! We have loads of candles and soft romantic lighting. Lewis is excited to capture the mood in there."

Alli led us inside and up the grand staircase to where several chairs were set up. Jeff occupied one seat and Beverly Turner another.

"Here you go. My other two guests," Alli said. "I've got to head back downstairs now. Enjoy!"

Jeff and Beverly were caught by surprise when Kim and I sat down next to them.

"Kim, no red dress this time, I see. Stay away from the stairs tonight," Jeff said.

"Haha. Very funny. Jackie and I were just talking about that night. I learned my lesson. I'm so glad Alli saw us standing outside. This is a dream come true to see a ball come to Harmony House again."

"What are you doing here, Jeff?" I asked.

"It was my suggestion," Beverly said. "I know he's been investigating the murder, and I thought this might be a chance to observe them in action. Instead of sitting across a table under those hot interrogation lights," Beverly teased, her hand resting on Jeff's thigh for a moment. "Plus, it gives me time to spend with local eye candy. Jeff reminds me of my friend Jeff Bridges. Don't you agree, Jackie?"

The blush that appeared above Jeff's denim shirt collar and rose to his cheeks was adorable.

"I've noticed that resemblance myself."

Jeff shook his head. "Stop now you all. Looks like the scene is starting."

Beverly leaned her body over to see better, brushing against Jeff's. "Yes, it is. As they say, quiet on the set."

I caught his eye and gave him an air kiss-kiss while he glared back at me.

CHAPTER FOURTEEN

he lights dimmed and filming began. We watched the action in the entryway below us. Couples mingled and chatted. Waiters carried champagne glasses on trays. Musicians tuned up.

The cameras focused on Eleanor, portraying her mother Constance Harmony, as she stood chatting with Josiah and Mary Bell. Dionne, acting as my mother Joanna, crossed in front of them. Josiah's eyes and the camera followed her. Then they reshot from another camera angle.

In the next scene Joanna stood watching the surrounding party. Her champagne glass rested lightly on the edge of her vivid red lips. Her eyes, soft and sexy, found Josiah just as Shayne aka Dad walked up to her and put an arm around her waist. Startled, she almost spilled her champagne. An expression of annoyance flitted over her face, before she softened her lips and turned to Dad with a smile.

Shayne was dressed not in a tuxedo but rather a suit just like I remember Dad having. One good suit. Dad was always uncomfortable in this sort of party environment but being next to Mom would have helped calm his nerves. I could well imagine my mother reveling in this environment. She was an elegant woman. Her carriage graceful. Her style impeccable.

Beverly was mesmerized by the scene too. I couldn't tell if her focus was the same as mine, or if she was a mother focused on observing her daughter.

As before, they shot the film from a second viewpoint. Lewis directed a subtle lighting change, moving Eleanor and the Bells to a different angle for another take of their conversation.

Then Alli motioned for us to come down, pointing to a place for us to stand and watch the next scenes.

A small band from Madison had been hired to play at the party and were set up at the edge of the solarium, in almost the exact spot where a combo had been the night Kim fell down the grand staircase.

"Will they play some Duke Ellington or Benny Goodman big band stuff? I love that," Jeff said.

"I agree," Beverly replied.

"Do you think their mustaches are real?" Kim asked. "They look pasted on to me. Won't they get in the way of blowing those horns?"

"I wouldn't worry about it. The musicians will most likely be faking most of their playing. For quality control, a digitized musical track will be laid over the musician's action. It's costly to record live audio in a setting such as this. And inconsequential to the value of the brief scene."

Beverly seemed to know her stuff.

Jeff's attention was on the film crew. His eyes scanned the room, watching them work, on the remote chance he'd learn something to help solve the murder.

"Are you happy they've added this scene?" Kim asked. "I know you, a movie star in Los Angeles, see parties like these all the time. Last time there was a gala like this here in Harmony I came in a stunning red dress. And so did the woman who was found murdered. She had the exact same dress as me. Can you believe that? You remember, Jackie, don't you?"

"I'm hardly a movie star, but my soap opera career has been very satisfying," Beverly said.

"And Kim herself ended up falling or being pushed down the stairs that night," Jeff said.

"Oh, now that would make it memorable. Sounds like the start of a good mystery. Same red dress on two women. One falls down the stairs and one murdered." Beverly winked at Jeff. "And you playing the investigator to solve it. Perfect."

"Oh, he didn't solve it. Jackie did," Kim blurted out. "Jeff even charged me with the murder! Can you believe it? Jackie is a dynamo crime solver."

"Well now, that's interesting," Beverly said, turning to look at me with a forced smile.

"Kim is right," Jeff said.

"That's gracious of you," Beverly said. "I'm sure you can solve murders. But I can't imagine you have many in this town."

"Wade may be the first murder of this year, but gosh last year we had how many?" Kim pinched her brow and touched her fingers one by one.

"Never mind, Kim," Beverly said. "I want to keep my illusions of the innocent and quiet existence you all lead here. Front doors left unlocked. Jail cells empty except for the occasional drunk."

"Mayberry, we're not." Kim was not dissuaded from the subject. "Why just last 4th of July we had two murders! One who drowned trying to get away from a fire. That wasn't technically the murder, but the fire was arson, and she couldn't swim. The person who set it knew that!"

"Kim, please. I don't think Beverly needs to hear

about our murder rate. Though it has taken a dramatic rise since Jackie returned to live here," Jeff said.

"Jeff! Stop! That may be true, but it has nothing to do with me," I scolded.

"Are you happy you moved back here from Chicago?" Beverly asked.

"Thrilled. I kept my loft in the city. But Harmony is my base now."

"You don't get bored? Miss all the restaurants and entertainment venues?"

"Maybe once in a while. But at my age, not so much. When I was younger, I wanted to leave. Get out of this small town. Explore other places. Use my photography skills around the world. But it's different now. I still enjoy traveling, but I'm always happy to get back home to Harmony."

"Don't think it would be for me. Alli's different. Not into the glitz and glamor Dennis and I used to enjoy. I've noticed it getting more tiresome lately. The small talk. Always trying to make connections for the next job," Beverly said. "Just a constant scramble. But when I was young, it was exciting. Now the expense of living a certain lifestyle in California is out of reach for so many young people."

"Like our daughter, except she has a wealthy mother to support her." Dennis had appeared out of nowhere to take Beverly's shoulders and give her air kisses on each cheek. "And I'm grateful for you doing that, darling."

Beverly cleared her throat. "Alli doesn't really need me. She's doing great without either of us."

"This is her first paid directing job. I hope the producer is paying her a generous salary," Dennis said, raising his eyebrows questioningly.

He shook hands with Jeff, asking if he was enjoying himself. "Or is this official business?"

"Just enjoying the company of these three lovely ladies."

"Who wouldn't?" Dennis quipped.

"I think Alli's looking for you to get started," Beverly quipped.

"Ahh, I'm being discreetly shuffled along." Dennis gave me a light kiss on the cheek. "So nice to see you again, Jackie. I hope we might do dinner before I leave town."

"Leaving so soon?" Beverly asked.

"I have a prior commitment back in LA. And like you said. Alli's doing fine without us."

"Will your new assistant Eleana be staying on?" Beverly's tone was snarky. "My accountant flagged an employment form from her just as the production end of things was wrapping up."

"I believe so. I only offered her the position after

Wade was no longer in the picture. No pun intended. He was covering her costs to travel with us. I didn't want to leave her stranded. Sorry, darling. I'm not taking enough salary here to cover it. If you want to take her off the payroll for the pittance she's making, feel free."

Beverly sniffed and turned her attention away from Dennis. He noticed and winked at Jeff, as to a comrade in the world of dealing with women, before walking away.

Even Kim was quiet after that awkward moment. But not for long. "Oh look, there's Ruth. OMG, she looks amazing. Oh, oh, and Betty. Wowzah! Val must have done their hair up-dos. They look great."

Quiet on the set was shouted out.

They filmed the couples dancing. Closeups of the band director doing his thing, the drummer rhythmically beating, and the trumpet player dramatically raising his horn. After consulting with Alli and Lewis, cameras and boom mics were rearranged.

Quiet on the set. Action.

Josiah and Mary Bell moved near my parents, who were doing an admirable swing dance. The couples smiled and spoke as they passed each other on the dance floor. When the music stopped, leaving the two couples standing near each other, my father accompanied Mary

Bell off the dance floor as Josiah bowed toward my mother. The music slowed.

"Here the camera shot will isolate them," Beverly whispered.

At first Josiah's hold was proper. From our position I observed his hand's formal position and light touch on Mom's back turn into an ever so subtle caress. Small move, but with it the audience would recognize everything that motion represented.

I glanced at Beverly. Her eyes were moist. Her posture stiffened. Like she was trying to hold herself together. Beverly Turner had seen it and felt it, too.

As soon as there was a break in filming, Beverly excused herself, saying she had a slight headache.

"Do you need a ride?" Jeff asked.

"No thank you." All flirtation was gone from her voice. "Good night."

Dennis watched his ex-wife leave. He tapped Alli on the shoulder and pointed it out to her. They both frowned and shook their heads. I saw the family resemblance in the gesture. I knew this was hard for Beverly. It was for me too. I hoped Dennis and Alli understood what she was going through.

"Was it something I said again?" Kim asked. "I thought she was enjoying this."

"I'm taking her at face value that she has a headache," Jeff remarked.

"Have you learned anything about a suspect or motive from watching all of this tonight?"

"I always like to observe and then digest what I've seen. Put it all into the entirety of my investigation."

"That sounds like a no," Kim said. "I'm keeping my ear to the ground for you though. Like did you know they are staying an extra day to reshoot some scenes downtown?"

"They are here longer? Maybe that means you can learn more," I said.

"I hope so. This is a tough one. So little to go on. I've reached out to the LA police to check on any records our system might not have picked up on. Guns registered, priors, stuff like that."

"Good idea. I'll let you know about anything more I can find out, Jeff. You know I can move like a stealthy panther when needed. Remember how I helped with that Victor Langdon case?" Kim said, straightening her shoulders.

Though I know he didn't want to encourage her, Jeff said, "Great, thanks, Kim. Hey Jackie, Kay and I were wondering if you and Scott want to join us for dinner tomorrow night. We were thinking of heading up to the

Wildwood. They have a fresh caught perch special going on now."

"I'd love to. I'll ask Scott." If he answers my phone calls, I thought. "On second thought, Jeff, why don't you ask him. And while you're doing that you might ask about Eleana. I think he took her out on his pontoon today. Maybe she confided in him about something."

"I'm getting all turned around here. I have a movie star hitting on me. And Scott is taking some young, cute assistant out on his boat. The world is flipping upside down."

"She was hitting on you. Ya' think?" I teased. "Maybe a little flirting, but I don't believe Kay has anything to worry about. Should she?"

"Whatever. I'm out of here. And all I'm saying is Hollywood coming to Harmony might not be all bad for us men." Jeff ducked away, avoiding my swing at him.

CHAPTER FIFTEEN

Dennis caught up with Kim and I when the crew began packing up to leave. "Why did Bev leave so suddenly? Is she all right?"

"I think watching the scenes where Josiah and our mom were courting got to her. It's surreal to me and I'm sure it is to her as well." As I spoke, I moved further away from Dennis. I needed no more special attention from him.

"She has struggled with that. I didn't know Bev when she found out she was adopted so I can't speak to those times. But she admits she hated her parents for not telling her. She acted out. Years later when she wrote her memoir it was cathartic for her. I encouraged her to write it, because after years of expensive therapy she hadn't worked through it. I know she tried. No big secret that it affected our relationship and was a part of our being divorced."

At that moment I felt empathy for Dennis. Just a touch. "Remember that Alli was the one who pushed Beverly to find her birth parents? Do you think that was wrong?"

"That took it up a notch for sure. But wrong?" He shrugged and blew out a long breath before continuing. "Not sure. Alli felt it was right to do. And she wanted her mom to get better too. With all the money Bev got from me in the divorce she can afford more shrinks. But enough of all this. Would you ladies like to grab a drink? I saw a little hole in the wall bar on Main Street."

"Shorty's!" Kim exclaimed. "That would be great. I'd love to. I'll let Stu know I'll be late."

I was less enthusiastic. Libby needed to be let out. But I rethought it as there was something I wanted to ask Shorty about. "Maybe a quick one, Dennis. I'll be here a few minutes yet, but will meet you two there."

"Kim, would you give me a ride? I came up here with the crew. See you over there, Jackie."

Alli saw me and ran over. "Did you enjoy it?"

"I did. Thank you for inviting us in. I'm so proud of my niece!"

"Listen, I only have a second, but I wanted to

mention that we'll be in town at least another day. There's some reshooting necessary."

"Oh. Bad for you. Good for me. I get to see more of you," I said. "What went wrong?"

"Marta discovered some questionable sections of film. We often do digital changes to scenes and audio tracks. Take something out. Adjust the sounds. Smooth over bra lines. Skinny up a body shot at an awkward angle. Innocent unremarkable trickery. But Marta said this is something bigger. She called it deceptive and wanted to show me, but I said let's just reshoot."

"Is this unusual?"

"I'm not experienced in that sort of thing. I've never been part of the editing. I just hope it's not infighting among the crew."

I reached to give her a hug. "You've got your dad to ask about this. He's super proud of your work. I'm sure it's a big learning curve."

"Thanks, Aunt Jackie."

I tried calling Scott about getting together with Jeff and Kay at the Wildwood tomorrow night, but again I got his answering machine. After leaving a message, I did my best at slamming the phone down by hitting the red hang up icon forcefully. There is something to be said for having a flip phone. With those you could do a satisfying snap shut.

I walked upstairs to where Aunt Ruth and Betty had changed out of their gowns and were chatting with Eleanor.

"What a special evening. You all looked beautiful."

"How'd I do portraying my mother?" Eleanor asked.

"You looked just like her, Eleanor. I remember that gown. She wore it to one of your weddings," Ruth said.

Eleanor grabbed her tummy in a belly laugh. "Yes, my weddings helped keep your sister-in-law in her dress business. You should have dressed up and been part of the evening soiree, Jackie."

"I'm too tall and gangly to fit in any of those dresses. But you have those perfect petite figures and looked like beautiful European aristocrats dancing the night away."

"It certainly will be interesting to see in the movie," Eleanor said. "This brought back so many memories."

A puzzled look crossed Ruth's face. "Now that I think about it, I don't remember my brother ever going to a ball here. Joanna would have wanted to, that's for sure. She loved to dress up and looked so glamorous when she did. Your father not so much. He had only one good suit."

"I was thinking the same thing about that suit when I watched him and Mom walk in tonight. I mean, watched Shayne walk in."

I smiled at the memory of Dad dressing up for

church, funerals, and weddings in that one gray suit. Mom would gift him ties from me for Father's Day so at least he mixed it up a little.

Ruth laughed. "I found myself doing the same thing. Mixing up the make-believe and reality. That was one handsome couple they found to play Joanna and Bob for this movie."

"Just like your parents were," Betty said to me. "But who told Alli that the Parkers would even come to a ball like this? Weren't they more common folk like my family? Back then a big night out meant going to Greensville for a drive-in movie."

Ruth and Eleanor both spoke at once saying they had asked Alli that very thing.

"But I thought you suggested it to her, Aunt Ruth? What did she say to that?" I asked.

"I did, but with the caveat it might not have happened that way. She implied someone encouraged her to add it as color. That it would improve the movie. That adding some juicy scenes would make these segments pop," Ruth said. "Sensationalism sells, I guess."

"Yes, it does nowadays," Betty said. "In the old movies things were different. Remember the twin beds in the master bedroom on the *Dick Van Dyke* show? Even kids then didn't believe that!"

Ruth chuckled. "Alli realized those trips to New York

and LA occurred at times when the seasonal fashion shows happened. She picked up on that herself. So, she might have wondered how the arrangements to meet were made, which led her to include these scenes."

"Good investigative work," I said. "Then the New York scenes weren't just about Beverly's early theater years there?"

"Right," Ruth said.

"It might be hard to think about all this. You were both so close to Joanna. But to be blunt, they did it somewhere," Eleanor said.

"Eleanor!" Ruth shrieked.

"She's right," I said. "I've often wondered how in a town this small there wasn't more gossip about their affair."

"As angry with your mother as I was, I am glad she kept it under wraps. As much as your father loved her, he loved you more, Jackie."

"And he was trying to spare me the hurt. I suppose that's what Beverly's adoptive parents felt they were doing too."

"I think I need to head home. Tom has been waiting for me. I don't want him to worry," Eleanor said. "See you all later."

Acts of love. My parents moved heaven and earth to keep us together as a family. Josiah spent endless efforts to find the daughter taken from him. Beverly's adoptive mother's love drove her to hide the truth. Between them, how much damage was done?

I heard Patti's voice giving direction on how the gowns were to be arranged. I poked my head in the room to see the silks and satins of evening gowns hanging from the modern headless mannequins used in the exhibit.

"Hey Jackie, I didn't know you were here!" Patti said when she saw me. "Did you see the filming? I'm so tickled that these beautiful gowns will get credit in the movie when it comes out. The Historical Society can use that to promote the collection."

Patti went back to showing the proper drape of the gowns to Connie.

"Did you hear anything that might help Jeff with his investigation?" I asked.

Patti raised a finger to her lip. "I sure did. We'll talk later."

CHAPTER SIXTEEN

*L*ibby was happy to be let out into my small, fenced yard in the alley before I headed over to the back door of Shorty's Tavern.

I entered and walked past the three guys playing pool and into the front of the bar where I found Kim and Dennis in an intense conversation with Shorty. The only open bar stool was next to Dennis. I slid it as far away from him as I could, but gaining only three more inches. Shorty set a Pulp Man Red Ale in front of me even as he kept his attention on the conversation with Dennis.

I tried to pick up the thread of what they were talking about. Something about a western film Dennis had directed. Something about tricking a sheriff.

"You're saying he was trying to fake the bail bondsman signature?" Shorty asked.

Dennis nodded. "For that movie I studied up on imitating signatures and initialing for verification. Forgery was a big part of how the outlaw tricked his way across the west. It was based on a great novel."

"I'll bet it's easy to learn," Kim said.

Shorty scribbled on a napkin and slipped it to Kim. "Here, Ms. Smartie. My initials. Try to copy it."

"I'd rather drink my wine. But okay, I'll try forging your initials."

"Interesting to hear all that. I think I've watched every movie you've directed. From spy thrillers to Westerns. But I don't remember that one with the forgery thing," Shorty said.

"It was in the *Bound for the West*," Dennis said.

"Oh yeah. Now I remember. Loved that movie. That almost broke up my marriage."

Shorty chuckled at my shocked reaction. "Made me want to move to Montana and live on the Blackfoot River. I had to have that cabin he lived in. Wife wasn't keen on the idea. Was it real or built for the movie?"

"Our site scouts found it and we leased it for the filming. The place sure was stunning. The locals worked with the actors, teaching them how to fly-fish on the Blackfoot."

"You ever been to Montana, Jackie?" Shorty asked.

"I've been to Glacier Park for a photography commission. Stunning scenery there."

"I'd love to go there one day before I die," Shorty said with a wistful look.

"A worthy goal. I have a friend with a cabin on the Blackfoot River. I'm sure he'd be happy to let you use it for a little fishy getaway with your buddies."

I almost reached over the bar to lift Shorty's jaw back up from where it had dropped.

"Seriously? Wow, I'd owe you one. Here, let me get you another drink. You're not driving, are you?" Shorty glanced at Kim who'd come in with Dennis.

"That lovely lady kindly gave me a lift here. But I'm walking the rest of the way back to the B&B I'm staying at."

Kim's head was still bent over the napkin and her tongue peeked in and out between her pinched lips.

Dennis turned to me as Shorty poured his drink, a scotch neat. I'm sure he'd asked for the best Shorty had. Thoughts of how old that scotch might be crossed my mind. Not in years of aging in a barrel, but time spent on the back bar here. This tavern saw little scotch poured.

"Glad you stopped in," Dennis said, resting his hand on my leg. I noticed Shorty saw the gesture but discreetly turned his eyes. This had to stop.

"Now Dennis, I know you are a Don Juan sort of person, but around these here parts ladies don't take kindly to cowpokes overstepping their bounds." I firmly took his hand and put it up on the bar.

Shorty flicked a wry grin my way as Dennis raised his hands in surrender.

"Don't shoot. I'm a stranger in a strange land."

He took a pretend cowboy hat off his head and held it against his heart. "My apologies ma'am. Didn't mean no harm."

"I didn't know my night would turn into a Dennis Turner western." Shorty grinned.

"Want to see my writing samples?" Kim asked, laying her napkin in front of Dennis and slapping it with her hand.

"Hmm?" Dennis studied the two samples. "Boy oh boy, Kim. You sure are close. But upon greater inspection…" He leaned toward Kim and began pointing out the obvious and not so obvious differences.

As he talked about elongated loops and tail lengths, I asked Shorty the question I'd been carrying around with me. "You once told me you had a crush on my mom."

"I did. Along with a lot of men, if I remember."

"Was she a flirt?"

"You mean like that one?" Shorty motioned toward Kim.

I had to laugh. He recognized it, too. "No. Kim just has it in her blood. She likes attention. I'm wondering if Mom was aware of the attention that came her way from men. This is so hard to explain."

"I get your drift," Shorty said. "There are the innocent flirts like Kim. She wouldn't know what to do if someone seriously hit on her. And there are the heavy flirters. The real come ons. I see those in here all the time. Then there are the non-flirters."

"Is that a word?" I asked.

Shorty shrugged. "I'm trying to describe a woman who is approachable in a friendly way but not a hint of impropriety."

"So back to my question about Mom."

"She was a classy lady. Aware of her beauty. But she never lorded it over anyone. Women can be jealous and unpleasant to each other. But Joanna was nice. Very nice. Flirty? Not that I ever saw."

"You know about her affair with Judge Bell?"

Shorty's gaze wandered around the bar before his eyes focused out his front window. With a deep sigh he said, "Guess most everyone does now."

"Did you know about it when it was going on?"

"Not a clue, Jackie. Not a whiff of it. I swear, it hit me in the gut when I heard. Could have knocked me over with a feather."

"Me too, Shorty. Me too."

"Why do you ask?" Shorty looked at me with sympathetic eyes.

"I feel like they have betrayed me. Not only Mom, but my dad and Aunt Ruth too. I wondered who all else in Harmony knew about it. Ruth claims it wasn't a big scandal."

"She's right. They kept it out of the gossip circles that exist in small towns. I don't know how, but it was a secret all these years." Shorty reached for my hand. "Your mother made a mistake. We all do. She did the best she could in the circumstances."

I squeezed his hand.

"Well now, that all sounds good," Kim said to Dennis, leaning back away from the napkins in front of her. "But I still believe a person could fake a signature given enough time. But I will not argue with you. You're way too cute and Shorty there is way too handsome to waste time on such trivial matters."

"Agreed," Dennis said.

"Right on, Kim," Shorty said. He raised his glass, and we all joined in. "Here's to *Becoming Beverly* being a successful record-breaking movie."

"Or at least breaking even for my ex's sake," Dennis added.

"Gotta run home to my cute cowboy now," Kim said with a wink.

"He's a lucky guy." Dennis gave Kim a kiss on the cheek.

Maybe he just did that to every woman. That made me feel a little better. I wasn't the only one he kissed.

"Good night, guys," Kim said as she left the bar.

"Careful getting home," Shorty called out. "You two want another drink? On the house."

"Nope, I'm good," I said, slipping off my stool and putting my purse on my shoulder. "Left my little Libby outside and she'll be waiting for me."

"Guess I'll call it a night, too. Jackie, could you walk me out front and point me in the right direction?" Dennis asked. "I'm not sure just which street is the best one to take back to my B&B from here."

Oh great. I hoped it was an innocent request, because I was tired and ready to snuggle in. By myself.

The moment we stepped outside we both saw Beverly standing in front of Vogue on Main staring into the large plate glass display windows.

CHAPTER SEVENTEEN

Dennis turned to me with a questioning expression. "What is she doing out here this time of night?" He stopped at the edge of the sidewalk in front of Shorty's and watched Beverly.

It was odd to see Beverly under the streetlight in front of the sign reading Vogue on Main. The street was quiet. No cars drove by. She stood alone, staring in the shop window.

"Probably still absorbing that this is the town her parents lived in. Worked in. Walked the streets. Led their entire life in," I said.

"Should we go up and talk to her?"

"You know her better than I do. What do you think, Dennis?"

"Let's go. She can always tell us to leave her alone."

Beverly still hadn't moved other than slight side-to-side tilts of her head. We crossed Main Street and approached her. I motioned Dennis to hang back a couple of steps before I walked up and stood next to her.

With a dreamy smile on her face she said, "Do you see her? Isn't she lovely?"

She?

Who was Beverly seeing?

Her own reflection?

But that wasn't it at all.

A wave of awareness hit me. I stopped a gasp from escaping.

"She is," I whispered.

Wind-tossed tree branches cast shadows against the plate-glass window. Between the eerie shadows mannequins revealed themselves. And there, between the mannequin wearing a soft pink day dress and the one in a crisp navy Chanel style suit, I saw her. The ghostly image of my mother. Looking back at me.

"I see her," I murmured.

"She's trying to reach us, isn't she?" The tiniest hint of a smile pulled at Beverly's lips. "How did this moment come to be? Decades after she gave us life, and years after her death?"

I had no answer. "Might she be asking for my forgiveness?"

"Maybe, Beverly." Shorty's words fell out of my mouth. "We all make mistakes."

"Am I a mistake? Has my whole life been a mistake?"

"That's not what I meant. Maybe I should have said everyone has things they…"

"Regret?" Beverly said. "Yes, we all have things we'd like a redo on. I know that all too well. But can I forgive her? Did your father forgive her?"

"He did," I said with less than complete confidence. But in my heart, and based on what Ruth shared with me, he must have forgiven her. He was not one to hold a grudge. Or regrets either. He'd always say life's too short.

"Do you think Josiah Bell forgave her for giving me away? For keeping me from him?" Beverly turned to look at me. "I imagine you've heard he searched for me, and that my birth parents kept his notes hidden. The three of them didn't want me to know."

"You've forgiven your parents. You must forgive Joanna too. For yourself and for Alli."

Beverly's hand reached for mine and gently squeezed it. "I suppose you're right."

She sighed and tipped her head toward Dennis. "That's what he always said. As you said, I forgave my mother and father for not telling me I was adopted when I was young. But there were years of my behaving atrociously after I found out they weren't my biological parents, such a cold term. Thankfully, they forgave me for that. I understood they were doing the best they knew. I just had to let it go. Then Alli stirred everything up and here we stand."

Dennis walked up to us and stood facing the store's window, too. "Alli needed to know," Dennis said. "She wanted to know. We were part of a different generation, Bev. Joanna did what she thought was best."

Beverly nodded. "Different times. Hmm…yes. They certainly were."

"And divorcees were treated differently. Look around at what she would have given up if she divorced. This idyllic little Hallmark movie town," Dennis said. "Her life here."

"Let me have this moment with my mother. Don't start in on all that about choices. Lifestyle isn't always what it appears to be."

Dennis bristled. "There you go. It's all about you. That's what it always was. I was just a vehicle for your ambition."

"Oh please. We were both struggling. You were just starting out yourself, but you had high ambitions."

"Ambitions aren't bad. You had them and did whatever it took to fulfill them."

"Can't you ever get beyond that?" Beverly spun and began striding away, leaving Dennis and I alone on Main Street.

Dennis reached for me. I didn't pull away. He needed a hug. This all was something they'd struggled with more than I knew.

"I'm sorry you had to hear that. She's right. I should get over it. Our divorce was bitter. She almost broke me financially. But I'll be okay, and we have Alli. It's been amazing watching her grow as a director. I'm grateful Bev wanted to make that dream come true for Alli."

Under his breath he muttered, "…and the means."

Never having been married and always having made my own way, I couldn't understand the feelings that must be involved in a divorce. But I was grateful knowing that my parent's marriage survived what my mother did. It gave me a wonderful life growing up in Harmony.

"I think I'll head home now, Dennis," I said, stepping back from him.

"Me too, Jackie. I'm sorry you had to hear all of this. What were the two of you staring at inside the store? Did Joanna's ghost make an appearance?"

I laughed. "Yes, she did. Did you see her?"

I hadn't noticed the large pickup parked down the street until it sped by, and I caught the words Drake Construction written on its door. My phone dinged.

I was going to surprise you. Guess I'm the one that got surprised.

"Whoa, guy's pushing way over the limit for this late at night. Bad news?" Concern showed on Dennis' face.

CHAPTER EIGHTEEN

reams of my mother were understandable. After all, I thought I saw her ghost last night. But when I woke up, any remnants of my dreams floated away. I tried lying still and letting them come floating back to me. It didn't work. Libby was literally pulling the covers off me. I'd better drag myself out of bed, before she rips up my bedding.

Did I see an actual ghost? I don't think so, but I'm going to talk to Patti about it. I'll bet Beverly and I were both seeing another mannequin further into the store. Or maybe the ghost was a reflection. Mirrors were mounted on interior walls. I could check that out as a plausible explanation. But then I realized I loved the idea of her spirit being with Beverly and I. Nope, I wouldn't try to find an explanation. I'd just remember that moment in time and be grateful for it.

My morning coffee smelled wonderful, but gray, overcast skies with dreary rain falling meant no sitting on my little balcony to sip it.

It also meant that filming other scenes would be delayed. At least my photography studio was being returned to its normal state today. The construction crew would show up to dismantle the 1950s Parker Photography and return it to my modern Parker Photography Studio and Gallery.

I tried calling Scott to explain that what he saw last night was not what he thought, yet again. But as was becoming a habit, he didn't answer. I knew full well he was by his phone. It was how he ran his business. I'm too old for such childish games. I didn't leave a message.

What he'd seen looked bad. I was in an embrace with Dennis Turner late at night on Main Street. But who was he to judge? He had been boating with Eleana earlier in the day. Of course, he'd asked me along. Was I sending mixed signals? Maybe I should get out of my defensive mode and try to explain. But how can you, Jackie, if he doesn't even pick up the phone?

I grabbed my windbreaker and umbrella, slammed my apartment door shut, and stomped down the stairs.

Before getting too upset I'd give Jeff a call and see if

he had reached Scott to confirm this evening's plans. Better yet, instead of calling Jeff, I'd walk over to the police station myself and let him know that I'd found out nothing from Eleana. That would get him off my back about the case. I'd again suggest Jeff talk to Scott about Eleana because he'd spent the day with her.

Fingers crossed Scott missed me as much as I missed him and our plans for a double date tonight were on. A dinner at the Wildwood would be something to look forward to.

But Scott wasn't pining away. Far from it. He and Eleana were sitting in one of the street side booths at Dolly's Diner. They were having breakfast together. And with Jeff! I couldn't believe it! Well good. Fine! Let them talk and figure it all out. I clenched my fingers around the umbrella handle, gritted my teeth, and shoved my head forward into the wind when, with a powerful gust, my umbrella reversed itself. The ribs bent up instead of down. The wind fought against me. An awkward struggle ensued.

Scott was probably getting a laugh at the sight of me battling with an umbrella and getting soaked. I stepped under an awning, righted the umbrella, and collected myself. I couldn't just stand here. I unexpectedly have the morning free. But where to?

I didn't have long to think, because I saw Mandy

waving and calling me from the Village Hall. Perfect. If Scott saw me walking past the diner and toward the Village Hall, he would assume I had a purpose to my day. That I wasn't just mucking about and waiting for him to call like some lovelorn teenager…nor an old lady being taken over by an umbrella. Mary Poppins came to mind, and I chuckled as I hurried toward the Village Hall.

"Morning, Jackie. Wasn't that amazing last night? I saw you up on the second-floor landing, but I was so busy capturing photos I didn't make it up there," Mandy said.

"Bet you got some great photographs."

"Alli had them up on Instagram this morning already," Mandy smiled. "I think that will be one of my favorite scenes in the movie. The glamor. The gowns. The music. I cannot wait to see this up on the big screen. I wonder where they'll have the grand opening. Maybe Graumann's theater in Hollywood?"

"I doubt it, Mandy. This might go to some film festivals, win some awards, and then be sold to one of the streaming platforms."

Patti and Dionne walked by. Their body language told me things were in a state of confusion right now. They stopped near us at the door in the front entryway and continued their discussion within earshot.

"And besides that, my dressing room floor is damp. Please have it taken care of. Where is Alli? I must talk to her. There isn't a call sheet up. This whole thing is leaving me stressed."

"I can help with the wet floor right away. Last I saw Alli she was in the screening room. You might check there," Patti said in a calming voice. But being her friend, I heard the tense undertone.

"I looked in there," Dionne snapped. "Marta was there, but that was all. This place creeps me out. Wade's ghost is lingering here." Dionne wrapped her arms around herself as though trying to control a shiver.

Patti raised her eyebrows toward me. Her haunted feelings were reinforced by a surprising source.

Flinging her arms back down, Dionne said, "And now the weather isn't conducive to filming so we're delayed another day. I have never been on such an unprofessional production. I'll have a word with Beverly. Thinking her daughter could ever handle a movie like this was crazy. If I wasn't such good friends with Beverly, I wouldn't even be here. She owes me a big favor."

"I will let Alli know you're looking for her," Patti said. "I need to get to work, myself."

Several of the crew, including Laura, the costume designer, were gathering in the large front entry. Two of the rented vans the production used waited outside. A young girl with a clipboard was checking names off.

"Have fun you all," Patti called out.

"Where's Chip? Did anyone see him? He's on my Taliesin list," the girl with a clipboard said.

"He's in the bathroom. You know him. Always with the sour tummy," Laura said.

A chorus of groans began. It switched into a rhythmic chant. *Chip. Chip. Chip.*

"Hilarious, guys," the missing crew member said, stepping out of the bathroom.

With more jostling and kidding the group loaded up in the vans.

"We were putting plans in place for them to move out today until Lewis and Marta discovered the outdoor shots on Main Street had to be redone. Now they are kicking back and making the best of the delay. I wish Dionne would do that," Patti said. "Did you hear she felt this place might be haunted, too?"

"I did," I answered. "I need to tell you about a spirit I may have encountered. But it can wait. What was it you wanted to tell me last night at the Harmony House?"

"No, please tell me now," Patti said.

"I thought you had to get to your office."

"I do. But you admitting you saw a ghost is worth a minute of my time."

Connie came hurrying up the basement steps with clothing hanging over her arms.

"Hey, Connie. Change of plans hah?" Patti called to her.

"Gotta stay nimble. Just learned about the reshoot for this afternoon if the rain stops. Or for tomorrow if not."

"Oh Connie, if you have a moment could you come to my office?" Patti asked.

"Sure, let me just run these things to the wardrobe trailer. I'll be right back."

"Jackie, I want Connie to be part of our conversation. Come in my office and shut the door."

"Our conversation? About what? The ghosts?"

"No, but I want to talk to you about a couple of things. First, I discovered that one key to the main door is missing or misplaced. I thought everyone was leaving today, and I was wrapping up loose ends. I gave two keys, on their big neon key fobs, to Alli. Alli gave one to Laura, the costume designer that first morning. You were here. Remember the stars' dressing rooms were being set up?"

"I do."

"Alli directed Laura to give it to Wade when she was done. Laura claims she did. But it wasn't in his personal effects," Patti said. "Maybe Marta borrowed it from him to work at night?"

"That's one thing I think Jeff could help track," I answered. "It is village property. He should know it's missing."

"True. I'd hate to change the locks but that would be an option. But the bigger question is why would it go missing?"

"Why do you think that's so important?"

"The janitor has his own key and comes in through the back-office entry near where the maintenance room is. When he arrived that morning, he remembered the common front door was locked as usual. So, whoever shot Wade had a key and locked the door behind himself when he left. The murderer had a key."

"Maybe the murderer took it off Wade's desk?"

"True. I hadn't thought of that," Patti said.

There was a knock on the office door.

"You wanted to see me?" Connie said, peering in.

"I did. Come in and close the door behind you," Patti said.

"Did I mess something up on the costumes last night?" Connie asked.

"No, nothing like that. I'd like to ask you to tell me more about what happened at that antique costume place you and Hannah went to. You said something about a problem with the company credit card."

"I don't want to be telling tales out of school." Connie nervously rubbed her hands.

"Look, I only want to know because I've recently discovered some questionable financial things myself. I started closing things up because you all were going to be leaving. Our account has open billings that should have been paid. Plus, the village was to get monies reimbursed for extra traffic control officers and it hasn't appeared yet. That reminds me, Jackie, did your check for the lease on your building go through?"

"I'm not sure. I guess so. Mandy handles the checking account, and I could ask her," I said.

Patti nodded. "Please do, Jackie." Then she turned to Connie asking, "This is not in your scope of work, but could you tell Jackie about that incident yesterday?"

Connie shifted uneasily. "I'm feeling uncomfortable talking about all this."

"I understand, Connie, but please, tell me again about the incident in Madison."

"When Hannah and I went to pay for the clothing we bought, they refused the company card. I didn't have a credit card of my own, so I called Beverly and she gave the store clerk one to use. It didn't seem like it was a big deal to Beverly though."

"And it probably wasn't, I just wanted to be certain I'd heard right. One more thing Connie, our police chief told me about you being the one who pinpointed the time of death. Could you tell me a little more about that?" Patti asked.

"Sure. I guess if he already told you I'm not telling any secrets."

Wait! What? I didn't know about Jeff having a time of death. Why didn't he tell me about it? I feel left out. But then I chide myself because that is what I wanted. To be left out of the investigation.

Connie continued with her story. "I didn't go to the party because I'd just been brought in by Laura that day. Besides, I'm not much for those sorts of parties. Laura had already put in a long day. She left before me. I wanted to get my head on straight about the shooting schedule and the costumes. I stayed later to bring myself up to speed and be ready for the next morning when my skills would be called on."

"Laura scheduled the shuttle van to pick me up in an hour. I finished in the wardrobe trailer and locked up. Then I found a bench in the park to relax and wait for the van. I had just sat down when I heard a shot fired. Figured us being in the Midwest, that sort of thing would be common, what with hunters and all."

"You weren't frightened? Or felt threatened?" Patti asked.

"Goodness no. Not here in this sweet little town.

When the van driver pulled up, I asked if he'd heard the shot. He pulled his headphones off and asked me what I'd said."

Connie chuckled. "I said forget it. He wouldn't have heard anything with the loud music coming out of those things."

"I know what you mean," Patti said. "I always warned my son to turn the volume down on his. So, you reported that gunshot sound when you heard someone had been murdered that night?"

"For sure. I knew it might be important. If it's okay, I'd like to get going now."

"Sure Connie, thanks so much for your help. Oh, one more thing. Have you seen a key on a bright neon green key fob?"

Connie shook her head, offering to ask around about it and left the office.

Patti saw my wheels turning and asked, "You getting the same feeling I have? Could this financial thing possibly have something to do with Wade's murder?"

"I don't really think so. I understand movies often come in over budget. I just can't tie it in with the murder. But the missing key might be a clue," I said. "You should go to Jeff about the key."

"Speak of the devil," Patti said, looking up toward her office door.

CHAPTER NINETEEN

"Me? A devil? Tsk. Tsk. That just isn't right. I'm shocked to hear you talking about me like that. And here I came because I felt you both sending out vibes of, *we need to talk to you, Jeff.* So, I walk on over and discover you speaking ill of me." He held his arms out, palms up. "What is this town coming to?"

"You read my mind, Chief. I want to talk to you," Patti said. "Pull up a chair."

Jeff took a seat and leaned back, clasping his hands behind his head. "Go ahead."

"I gave keys to Alli. It would make access to the building easier and more convenient for their sched-ules," Patti said.

"Yes, I know of those. We talked about them the

morning the body was discovered."

"One of them is missing."

That got Jeff's attention.

Patti continued. "Alli gave one to Laura. I talked to her today, and she said she gave it to Wade as Alli had directed her. I heard you did not find it in his things."

"Who told you that?"

"Murph did. I called him when I discovered Alli didn't have it. He said it wasn't in the editing room or Wade's room at Kay's B&B. I'll be asking around more about it, but Jackie thought I should let you know as it might be a clue. Plus, the front entry door was locked, so whoever shot Wade left by that door and locked it behind them. The only other keyed door is one in the rear that the janitor has his own key for."

Jeff sat up and leaned over toward me. "You are involving yourself in this investigation after all? Thought you said you wanted to be hands off."

"I do. Patti was telling me some things, and I made a simple suggestion is all, as a friend."

"You are a good friend. I heard your friendship and maybe a bit more, extends to the director in town."

"Alli's my niece, Jeff. You know that. Family means a great deal to me."

"I meant the other director. Dennis Turner."

Patti's eyes flew open. "Jackie? Seriously? Not him. He's not your type."

Ugh! "Jeff, you've been talking to Scott. Don't believe what he's telling you. He's got it all wrong."

"So, I shouldn't believe what he told me about Eleana either? Did I just waste an hour talking with her? Darn. Who can you trust?"

"No, not that. May I remind you that you begged me to see if I could find out anything about her? Scott and she ended up spending the day together on the pontoon boat."

"What on earth is going on?" Patti exclaimed. "Scott and Eleana? You and Dennis?"

I rolled my eyes at Patti. "It's not like that. I'll explain later. First, I want Jeff to finish telling us about Eleana."

"Now it's us. You wash your hands of helping me figure out her part in this drama. You say don't bring me into another murder. And now you want to know what I found out. My oh my but I am one confused police officer," Jeff said. "But okay, since you insist. Scott gained Eleana's confidence. She trusted him enough to confide all she knew about the murder situation."

Jeff explained that Eleana and Wade had been engaged. She'd given up her career in LA to travel with him during the making of this film. Things began falling apart between them. When they were booked in the same room at Kay's B&B, Eleana knew she couldn't stay with him and made plans to go back to LA. But she was stranded financially. Dennis felt bad for her and offered to hire her as his assistant until everyone got back to LA."

"That all happened the night they got in? The night before the party at the Stone Mill?" Patti asked.

"Right. Did either of you see Eleana at the party?" Jeff asked. "What was she acting like that night?"

"She wasn't happy. I overheard her asking one of the guys where Wade was. A group had just arrived on Matt's pontoon, and it seemed like she was expecting Wade to be with them. The guy blew her off and said he's your boyfriend. How should I know where he is? She was mad, even asking if he was with someone else. The guy spun around to get away from her and bumped into me. His drink sloshed out on her sparkly blue dress. I learned later that she left to go back to the village with Matt on the pontoon."

"She must enjoy boating on pontoons," Jeff joked. "I'm going to get the specific times Matt left Stone Mill and arrived back at the marina."

Patti told Jeff that she saw Matt leave the dock that night at about eight o'clock so he would have gotten to the marina about a quarter after.

"If that's correct, she was in the area at the time of

the murder and had a motive," Jeff said. "I have my suspicions about her. But about the gun? Just doesn't fit. Did Alli go back on the pontoon also?"

Now that the timeline of the murder was tightened, Alli had an alibi! I breathed a sigh of relief and said, "No, she didn't. I talked to Alli shortly after she and Dennis convinced Eleana to take the pontoon back to town."

"I don't know where this fits in, but there is something up with the finances of Turner Productions," Patti said.

"And you're thinking again, like with the key, it's something I should look into?" Jeff asked.

"Yes," I said. "And have you done any handwriting comparisons on that note?"

"Whoa. Slow down, everyone. The Turner Productions money problems don't raise flags for me, but thanks for letting me know. I'll reach out to Alli and her mother and get a better picture of the financial situation. And yes, I have checked on the note and I believe I know who wrote it."

"Who is it?" I asked.

"If you want to know all about my investigation, maybe you should come with me. I'm going downstairs to question Marta right now," Jeff teased.

"I'll go along and ask her about the key," Patti said.

I hesitated. My primary concern had been that my

niece possessed what could have been the murder weapon. But now that she had an alibi, I could step away from all of this. Let Jeff and Patti talk to whomever they wanted to.

Deciding I had better things to do, I was saying my goodbyes when the sound of raised voices came up from the basement offices. Among the escalating shouting, the only word I understood was Alli. I knew I had to go down and find out what was going on. All this turmoil was messing with her chance to make a great movie on her first time out as a director.

I hoped Jeff wasn't getting the wrong idea about why I changed my mind. I heard his snicker and shot him a side-eye as he followed me to the basement.

CHAPTER TWENTY

Dionne had her face right up in Alli's. "You can't handle this. I'm taking it to your mother." She spun around and pushed past us, flouncing up the stairs.

Alli's shrug showed me she was unruffled. "Dionne's a family friend. She practically owes my mother her career. Mom will straighten things out. I'm more concerned about the others in there. I need to figure out why they are at each other's throats. This rain delay is making everyone grumpy."

The *they* she referred to turned out to be Lewis and Marta. They argued, gesturing, and pointing to images up on several of the computer screens in front of them.

"Are you okay, Alli?" I asked. "If there's anything I

can do, please let me know. You must be under so much pressure."

"Thanks, Aunt Jackie. What are you guys doing here, anyway?"

"Couple of questions," Jeff said. "But first, why don't you step in there and settle them down. We can wait out here."

"I'm glad you're here," Jeff whispered to me.

"I'm just here to support Alli," I whispered back.

"Understood." Jeff nudged me. "She's a lucky gal to have you help her."

"There. Right there." Lewis jabbed his finger at the screen. "I had the perfect light angle for the shot. And now it's ugly. What the heck is going on here?"

Alli stepped up to the workstation where Marta sat to do her editing. "Lewis, calm down. Let me see what you're talking about."

"Alli, you must remember this scene we shot in New York. The light, the mood, the atmosphere. All perfect. Now it's ruined. Someone has been messing with the film again. I do not create work like this. My reputation will be ruined," Lewis whined.

"I remember that shot. It gave me goose bumps when

I watched it. Rewind it to the point where Rod walks out from under the hotel awning," Alli said.

The three of them silently watched the video as Jeff and I looked through the open doorway.

"Now do you understand?" Lewis said. "It's awful. It's been tampered with to reflect poorly on me."

"Don't be silly," Marta said. "Why would I do that? Let me check the time of last viewing and see if it might have been altered then. Maybe we can get the original back and sub it in."

Marta pulled up the image on a different screen and began typing on the keyboard. Her actions produced data scrolling on the screen. "It seems like it was pulled up three nights ago."

"You were here that night," Alli said. "Was Wade making you change something?"

Marta pushed back from the desk and threw up her hands. "Why on earth would I alter the film? Why would Wade make me do it? Are you kidding me? This is crazy talk."

"Then who was in the system and looking at this scene?" Alli asked.

"It's happened before too. I haven't rewatched all the scenes, but I smell a rat," Lewis snarled.

"Please tell me what you two did that night," Alli said.

"Nothing. He wanted me to meet him, as he had a

couple of ideas that he thought wouldn't wait until later, and he said he needed my help with the equipment. He was that way. You know the guy, Alli. Demanding. Arrogant. The door was locked when I got here so I never saw him."

"Liar." Lewis tried to push Marta's chair back from the editing board.

"Stop it right now." Alli's voice took on an authoritative tone. "Could Wade have done this digital manipulation himself?"

"I don't think so," Marta said. "It's complex. He wouldn't have that knowledge of this system."

"Oh yes he could have," Lewis said. "He was a film editor way back when. He rarely talked about it though, because his passion was directing. Didn't you know that, Marta?"

"Then why did he ask me to help with even the simple things?"

"Good question," Jeff said, as he and I entered the room. "Why would he have written that note asking you to be here, Marta? Or did you write the note to him?"

Marta's eyes grew wide. She took a deep swallow. "Note? I wrote a note, sure. I left it right here on the desk. He saw it and texted me to meet him."

She reached for her cell phone and scrolled down the

screen. "Here, this is the text I got. He found the note and said eight was fine."

Jeff read the text and handed the phone back to Marta. "So where did you go after discovering you couldn't get into the building?"

"I had gotten here a couple of minutes late. When I discovered the building locked up, I figured he'd left or stood me up. Plus, my eyes were still bothering me. You know that, Alli. I borrowed your contact solution. I didn't want to go out with everyone because my eyes were burning. I went back up to my room."

"Can anyone vouch for your whereabouts during the time between eight and nine?" Jeff asked.

"Are you accusing me of killing Wade?"

"Please, ma'am. Can someone vouch for your where-abouts that night? Maybe there was someone in the park?"

"There was! Someone was walking past. She'd come from the direction of the marina."

"That could have been Eleana, based on the time they left on the pontoon," I said.

CHAPTER TWENTY-ONE

Jeff asked Patti and me to come back to his office with him.

"Can't I just talk to you here, Jeff? I've got stuff to do in my office."

"Please, Patti. It's important," Jeff said. "I'm asking nice. And Jackie, I'll lure you over there with a message from Scott."

When we were seated in Jeff's office and he'd given us cups of steaming hot coffee to take the chill away, he got down to business, pulling out a pencil and a small notepad.

"I need to hear more details from the night of the party. Jackie, you told me about how Eleana talked to the guy at the bar. She was aggravated at that point. And that was before she got on the pontoon to go back to town."

"I don't know about the timing, but yes, she was in a bad mood, and she walked away with a martini in her hand," I said. "But within a few steps she stumbled, and the glass broke. Dennis and Alli appeared at her side and took her outside on the patio. They would be the ones to talk to about that time."

"I have spoken to them both, but I want to hear from all witnesses," Jeff said. "That was the last time you saw her that night?"

"Not quite. I saw her getting on the boat and Matt pulling away from the dock."

Jeff turned to Patti. "Did you see or hear anything involving Eleana during the time before she left the party?"

"Charlie and I had a table on the patio. We overheard some of the conversation when they brought her outside. I remember because she was making quite a scene," Patti said. "She appeared overwrought and was bending Dennis's ear saying she wouldn't be stuck in this hick town alone if not for Wade. I could kill him for what he's putting me through. I should be the director's fiancé, not the pretend assistant to the ghost director. Dennis convinced her to go back with Matt and helped her down the stairs. That's when you came out, Jackie."

"Sounds right, because I talked to Alli then."

"I'm down to two suspects. Marta and Eleana. Alli was high on my list as she admitted to having a gun. But now she has a rock-solid alibi. Knowing Marta was with Wade that night and at the scene where they found his body, that puts her front and center."

"Hold on," I said. "She just told us she didn't get in the building. That the door was locked."

Jeff raised one eyebrow. "She also seemed sketchy on her alibi. I'll be putting all these things on a time-line this afternoon and see where the holes are. Now as to Eleana, I sure am taking a tougher look at her after hearing she threatened to kill him. Geez, unbelievable. Neither Dennis nor Alli told me that. Did they forget?"

"What motive for Marta though? And how could she have stolen the gun out of Alli's room?"

Jeff reached out for a small notebook lying on his desktop. "You just heard her say she borrowed contact solution. That meant she had been in Alli's room. Alli and I went over who could have taken her gun, but she seemed confused because it was soon after the murder. She never tried to hide that she carried it with her. She said Eleana stayed there for about an hour after she argued with Wade. Of course, Kay and the cleaning staff would have had keys to the room. But that's all she could think of. I'm going to interview her again when she's cleared her mind."

"And you're confident about the woman who heard the gunshot?"

"Yep. I tested it with Murph. He fired a gun in the same space, while I sat on the bench Connie had been waiting on. I heard it," Jeff said.

"There's only so much you can do. It sounds like it must be one of the two. Neither has a solid alibi and one has a motive. Marta might as well. If Wade accused Marta of digitally manipulating the film to make him or Alli look bad, that might be enough motive."

"I don't have good proof on either one, Jackie. They'll all be leaving town soon."

"Maybe I'll find the missing key and that might provide another clue," Patti offered.

"True. It might prove to be the important missing piece I'm looking for. Now you know where I'm at. If you could kick that mind of yours into high gear, I'd sure appreciate it."

I couldn't shake a niggling feeling I had that we were both missing something.

"What did Scott say about dinner with you and Kay tonight?"

"We're all set," Jeff said. "I don't know what's been

happening between you two, but Scott was glowing when he left the diner and knew he'd see you tonight."

"Ah yes, the diner. I saw the three of you in there this morning."

"And we saw you. Valiant effort against the rain and wind. But it looked to us like the umbrella won."

CHAPTER TWENTY-TWO

*B*ack at the studio Kirsten was straightening things up. "They just finished up repainting the walls and said I should avoid getting things too close, so I don't mess up the fresh paint. Oh, and they asked if we'd review the positioning of the security camera. They bumped it and wanted to alert us it might not be aimed in the exact direction as before. We will have to confirm the computer cords are connected properly to the register and all that. Mandy said she'd have Matt come over and handle that. You should have seen how fast they got things back into place. Just need to readjust the display panels."

"Glad our place is done. It's distracting not to have things in order the way we're used to," I said. "The older

I get the more I need order. I feel discombobulated without it."

"I don't know how these people travel and keep everything straight. I have a new appreciation for the work that goes into making a movie. One carpenter here said all this work and it might only be in the movie less than a minute," Kirsten said.

Now that I knew things were under control here, I decided to go to the wardrobe trailer to talk to Laura about that key. Since the outer door at the Village Hall was found locked, the murderer had to have the key. Laura had the key in her possession at one time. The idea she could have made a duplicate was possible. I needed to ask her myself and to watch her body language when she answered if the key really had gone back to Wade.

The rain hadn't let up but a surprise text from Scott brightened my day. *Looking forward to dinner tonight xo*

I returned his message in all caps *ME TOO.*

When I arrived at the trailer only Laura was there. I offered some chitchat about Taliesin to put her at ease. She said she enjoyed it but didn't do the outside part of the tour because of the rain. She continued sorting garments as we talked.

Laura assured me she had given the key to Wade after that first morning of setting up the dressing rooms.

She asked why I was asking after it as she'd already told Patti and Jeff what she knew.

"It's just a key. Can't they make another one?"

I laughed. "True. Patti's just trying to avoid having to change the locks."

"Midwestern practicality. I can't imagine who else Wade might have given it to. Maybe the murderer took it from him."

"That's a thought," I said. "What made you think of that?"

"I watch lots of *Law and Order* shows," she said.

"Or maybe someone had a duplicate?" I suggested.

She didn't flinch. "Possibility. You should ask at the hardware store. I remember it had an unforgettable fob and surely whoever cut the key would have noticed it. When I was young, we used to have those on gas station bathroom keys."

"I remember that too! The bathrooms were always outside the station."

"And not pretty."

"Ooh and the smell. Yech!"

"Did you ever think there was a peep hole in there? I used to have nightmares about that," Laura said.

"Traveling is nothing like that now, thank goodness. All the hotels, restaurants, and conveniences along the way. Is Connie around?"

"She just left. The van took her to the airport to catch a flight back to her home in New Jersey. We didn't need her help any longer. But she sure filled in and helped on short notice."

"Were you with her when she heard the shot?"

"No, I had left earlier because it had been such a long day. That was quite something wasn't it. Did it turn out to be an important clue?"

"Sure did. Since you watch *Law and Order,* you know about the time of death being given as a window of time. Since she heard the shot at 8:22 p.m. exactly, it pinpointed it for our Chief of Police."

A look of concern crossed Laura's face. "Oh no! Is that what she told him?"

"What's wrong? Was it a different time?"

"I can't be sure, but I think Connie never changed her watch from East Coast time! We shared a room at the Riverview, and I noticed it. She said it had been her mother's watch, and the stem was fragile. It worked to rewind the watch, but not to pull out and change the time. I can't believe she didn't remember that when she talked to the police. Oh my god! This means it's an entire hour off. But still in the window of time the medical examiner said, right? I mean she's a little spacey, but a skilled seamstress."

I couldn't believe what I was hearing. Could this

have happened? "Laura, if what you're saying is true it changes everything. Yes, it's in the window of time, but our chief is investigating with that very specific time in mind. Didn't Connie have to be on time everywhere?"

"Connie was doing me a huge favor. She's retired but agreed to help me. I took her under my wing, getting her where she needed to be. I would have had to do everything myself here in Harmony because Beverly took away my other wardrobe assistant after New York. She said there was so little costuming to handle here. I didn't want to argue, so I covered Connie's travel and her salary, hoping I'll get reimbursed."

Those words again. The finances. The budget.

"Would you mind if I went with you to talk to Jeff, our Chief of Police, and you can tell him your story? Maybe he can call Connie and confirm what you're saying. I've got a feeling it will be important. Very important."

"Of course. Let's do it right now."

After Laura left the police station, Jeff put a call in to Connie. Her husband said she wasn't home from the airport. He knew about her not changing the time on the watch. Her mother passed away recently, and he'd noticed she wore the watch every day. He ended the call saying he would have her call back.

Jeff rubbed his chin. "Oh boy. This changes things. It gives Eleana an alibi but still not Marta. No one saw her walking up to or entering the B&B."

Neither of us spoke.

We were both thinking the same thing.

This made Alli a suspect.

CHAPTER TWENTY-THREE

It didn't take long for a call from Connie to come in. Her daughter picked her up at the airport and had gotten the message. Jeff put the phone on speaker. Connie confirmed that the time she reported was incorrect. I heard her apologizing profusely and berating herself for mixing that up. She hoped it didn't mess up his investigation. Jeff assured her he'd work around it and told her it helped confirm someone's alibi. Even as he was saying this, I could see how upset he was to have spent all this time on wasted efforts. He was clenching his jaws and shaking his head side to side.

"Jackie, I owe you big time. If not for you being willing to help Patti find the key, we might never have gotten the correct time of the murder."

"It would have come out eventually, but thanks. Pretty crazy how this happened."

"You have a certain magic detective touch."

"No, I don't. Don't be goofy. It just was a matter of it falling into my lap. Kay was at the party so she couldn't have seen when Marta arrived back that night. It could be Marta too, right Jeff?"

"But she told us she was meeting Wade at eight and found the door locked," Jeff said.

"Maybe she went to meet Wade an hour early. Surprise him. She could have kept the text to prove the time of the meeting, but all along knowing she'd go over earlier. Remember, she was in Alli's room getting contact solution, so she would have had access to the gun as well."

"True, Jackie. I'll have to interview them both again now that the time of the murder has changed. Pretty random that Laura brought that up with you, isn't it? The key is still an issue though. We know Alli had one for sure."

"But Marta could have just taken it from Wade's desk if she went early. Killed him and left, locking the door behind her. There's someone else I'd think about, Jeff."

"Who's that?"

"Laura. She had the key at one time. Easy enough to get a duplicate made, or maybe she never returned

Wade's. I think she argued with Wade and Alli about money because she felt she was understaffed. I just learned that she was paying Connie out of her own pocket because money was so tight. She said she was hoping to get reimbursed when all this settled down. And I don't think she would have an alibi for the time of the murder. She left Connie working by herself that night."

"I don't know about that idea. I mean thanks for offering it up, but Laura seems lacking a serious motive. Much less the means. Alli never mentioned her having access to the gun. I just don't see it there on her end. Seems too far removed."

Jeff pushed back from his desk and said, "Marta might still be at the Village Hall. I'll head over there and talk to her again. To me she is the stronger candidate. Motive and means. Now with the time change let's see what she comes up with as far as an alibi."

"And Alli? Is she a suspect now too?" I knew what his answer was going to be. I dreaded hearing it, but I would have to face it.

"I'm afraid so, Jackie. She told me she was at that party at the original time of the murder. But now it happened earlier. You said she showed up about 7:30 p.m. looking frazzled. She had the means. She's the only person close to the case that had a gun."

"But she didn't have a motive, Jeff. Why kill her assistant director?"

"Good point. I don't know everything, but between the Lewis and Marta argument we witnessed, and the financial issues Beverly is dealing with, there is obvious tension in the Turner Production company. Lots to chew on. As to Alli, she looks more stressed every day she's been here."

"Not stressed like she'd just murdered someone, Jeff. She's been working hard and is exhausted."

"Want to come with me to the Village Hall?"

"In case you charge my niece with murder?"

"Jackie, you're not being fair. I'm not going there to charge her with murder. I'll be talking with both Marta and Alli. This is my job, Jackie. I like Alli, and I'm going to assume she has an alibi for the new time of the murder. I'm not going to arrest her. She's certainly not a flight risk. My job is to solve the case with enough evidence to prosecute. So, want to come along?"

"No, I will not go with you, but I will be interested to find out what you learn. There are a couple of things I need to attend to."

"We can talk at dinner tonight."

"Okay. Sounds good. See you later."

The pressure for me to help just kicked into high gear. Especially because I'm the one who turned in the clue that changed the time of the murder and put Alli in Jeff's crosshair. I can't let my niece handle this on her own. I need to talk with Beverly about the money situation, but I'm not sure how to approach her. Should I let her know her daughter might be charged?

CHAPTER TWENTY-FOUR

hankfully Beverly agreed to meet me at Murphy's coffee shop. We sat at a small table under the window, the rain pattering against the glass next to us.

She thanked me for crossing the street to talk with her last night. "I'm sorry if I seemed kind of crazy. But I've never felt such a thing. I think I have a new appreciation for ghost hunters. How did you and Dennis end up showing up there together though?"

"He and Kim met with me for a drink at Shorty's. Our local little tavern. Just a spur-of-the-moment thing."

"Ah yes. My ex. I imagine he was in hog heaven sipping a scotch between two lovely ladies. I suppose he's hit on you at some point during his time here."

I had to chuckle. "I think he may have been trying, but not in earnest. But I'm not interested in him. A very handsome, charming man, but not my type."

"Do you have a type, Jackie? I have several," Beverly said with a wink.

"My type is now Scott Drake. I'd love for you to meet him someday. Maybe tonight? We're meeting Kay and Jeff for dinner. I'm sure they'd love it if you joined us."

"I didn't know Jeff and Kay were a couple. Now I'm embarrassed about my behavior toward him last night," Beverly said.

"He's a good-looking man. No one could blame you. He's devoted to Kay, but I know he appreciated your attention."

"I'm considering leaving town this afternoon. With this miserable rain delay I'm feeling a bit dreary being here. I need some warm California sun. What was it you wanted to talk about?" Beverly asked.

"You can just say it's none of my business if you want, but I have some questions about the financing of this film project, and you seemed the best person to ask."

Beverly's gaze turned toward the village green glistening with rain drops. She raised her cup to her lips and took a small sip. "Ah that. Yes. I'm afraid I'm indulging my daughter's dream by putting up the money for the project. Was I wrong for doing that?"

When I began to speak, Beverly shook her head. "It was a rhetorical question, Jackie. Only I can answer it. But I'm learning things both about Alli and about making a movie. I'm actually quite impressed with her directorial capabilities. However, I can see she fell short on her budgeting estimates. But in her defense, it's difficult to estimate costs because unforeseen events, like this rain delay, pop up. I would have the money to cover any overages, but I think the better lesson would be for her to have to learn about the true cost. Dennis and I have butted heads on this in the past. Neither of us has produced a project and here I sit with a startup production company. He's a terrific director, but not at all business minded. I'm an actress and have always been careful with my money. Yet another thing to thank my parents for. But I ramble. What were your questions?"

Did Beverly know Alli allowed Wade to approve expenditures? She didn't mention it, so I let it drop for the time being. "I've heard there have been some issues with payments and cash shortages."

"Who did you hear that from? Crew gossip, I suppose. Movie and television sets are notorious for that. And why does it involve you?"

"I wouldn't have given it a second thought except I'm concerned about Wade's murder."

"What on earth would a movie budget have to do with his murder?"

I sensed I was stepping a little too far into things with Beverly. I had no clear-cut reason to think this had anything to do with his death. I should just drop the whole thing.

"Jackie, I asked you a question."

The temperature of our conversation cooled.

"Right. Beverly, how closely do you follow the bills that come in? Or do they go right to your accountant?"

Beverly frowned. "Please don't answer my question with a question. What does this have to do with the murder? Obviously, we are all concerned and are hopeful they will solve it. But you seemed to imply that the money trail has something to do with it. Am I missing anything?"

Okay, back off, Jackie. But the words tumbled out. "Could money be a motive for his murder?"

Her lips pulled back in surprise. "No. What a stupid question, Jackie."

"It's not stupid. Money is often a motive."

"Well not in this case. Wade had no money to speak of. Who would murder him for money? Except maybe that trollop he had with him. She loved the exciting life of Hollywood. All the glitter. Lights. Fancy cars. But she hitched herself to someone who was grabbing for the brass ring and missing it. If you'll excuse me, I'd like to find my daughter and say goodbye. I've decided to leave early."

"Beverly, I'm sorry if I said something wrong. I was hoping we could get to know each other a little better."

"Perhaps another time. Maybe you'd enjoy coming out to LA one day to visit." Beverly put money on the table. "I need to help Alli work through this process and get *Becoming Beverly* out of production and onto the screen. That's part of my job as a producer. It's been stressful for me, and it has nothing to do with what you suggested. Bye now, Jackie."

I accepted her kiss-kiss as a curtain dropped between us. She left, popping open her umbrella as soon as she stepped outside the door.

"That didn't go well," I murmured, as Grace Murphy, the proprietor approached my table.

"So that's your sister? She's beautiful, just like you," Grace said.

"She is a gorgeous woman. Much more glamorous than me."

"But you have an inner glow I don't see in her," Grace said, picking up our coffee cups. "I sensed the mood changed during your conversation. Is everything okay?"

"You sensed right. I pushed too far and hit a sore spot for Beverly," I said. "Thanks for asking. Maybe I'll have to find another way to get answers."

"I've met some of the other actors. Even took photos with them," Grace said.

"Thinking of starting a wall of fame, are you?" I teased.

"Oh my no. We don't get many famous faces here. I'm perfectly happy with the smiling locals any day. But my sister in Ireland knows Rod Jessup and the young girl who played you as a child. Forgot her name, but anyway I thought I'd send them to her. So easy to pop photographs off as an attachment now."

"Isn't that true? Lot fewer photographs printed up now though. All stored digitally."

"I thought about brightening the photos up a little, but I don't have the patience or skill for it. She'll have to take their faces as is, warts and all." Grace's cheerful lilting laugh made me smile.

It was true. With modern technology it was easy to manipulate everyday photographs. Was that all that Wade was asking Marta to do? Or was it more?

Jeff's patrol car was still parked in front of the Village Hall. That meant I couldn't talk with Alli yet. She might have a take on the finances that her mother didn't. I wished her mother would stay here to be with her if things went south fast. Maybe Dennis will stay in town. He and Alli seemed to have a closer relationship.

Since it looked like I'd have to wait to talk with Alli, I went back home to get ready for my evening out with Scott. It would be a wonderful escape.

CHAPTER TWENTY-FIVE

"Watching paint dry on a rainy, humid day is not my idea of fun." Todd sat hunched over the sales desk with a glum expression on his face.

"I'm surprised to see you here. I thought Kirsten was in all day. What's wrong?"

"She forgot she had to take an online test."

"And that makes you this unhappy?" I asked.

"Alli promised me an hour of her time for an interview. And I was planning on taking her up to Timbers Grill. Maybe make those plans to visit her in Los Angeles. But she's tied up. All she could say was maybe later today."

I'd seen him chatting with Alli and watching her

work over these past few days. He should know that she's not avoiding him.

"Todd, there's a good reason for her not joining you just yet. There's been a major change in the murder investigation and Jeff needed to talk with her."

"What happened?" Todd sat up straight. "Is she okay?"

"She's fine. But Jeff learned the time of the murder was not what he thought. He was given erroneous information. Now he needs to talk with those involved and ask additional questions. She's with him and some of the staff at the Village Hall right now."

Todd breathed a sigh of relief. "Well that supersedes our plans for sure. This has been weighing heavy on her. Also, her mother has been pressuring her about the financing. And now with Wade gone, she's had to handle it alone. She mentioned that she hasn't had time to go through the books in detail like the accountant and her mother want. I hope this new information clears up the case and Jeff can find the killer, so things can get back to normal for Alli."

"Me too," I said. But I left it at that. After all, Marta was under suspicion too. There was no need to bring up hypothetical scenarios.

"Did the paint dry under your watch?" I asked. I don't know if Todd realized I was choosing to change the subject because it bothered me to think about the possibility of Alli being charged with murder. I thought not being there with Jeff during the interviews would get it off my mind. Distract me. But it wasn't working.

Todd stood and reached to tap the painted wall with his fingertip. Pulling it away and holding it up toward me he said, "Looks like it did. Good. Now I can finish moving the display panels back instead of having to come back later."

"There you go. A positive outcome to your date being delayed. Kirsten gone for the day then?"

"Yep. She told me a couple of things to let you know. They moved the security camera aim back, but she left it recording until you can confirm it's the original angle. There's an email message from that photographer in Gulf Shores you might want to respond to sooner than later. And…" Todd looked down at a written note. "A package was delivered, and it's in the back."

"I hope that package contains the new treats I ordered for Libby. She's been gaining weight. I'll take a peek at the security camera video footage. I'm so glad Mandy suggested taking photographs of how the things on the wall were arranged. It will make them much easier to rehang. Can you remind me how to pull the video up on the computer?"

When I tapped the keyboard, the screen opened up

to a photograph of the editing room in the basement of the Village Hall.

Todd looked over my shoulder. "Mandy did a great job with the social photos."

"But why is this photograph of the video editing room up?"

"She was playing with working on removing Wade from the earlier photographs. Alli wants to give the crew a gift photo book and she thought it might be better to remove Wade from most of them and just do a memorial type of page at the beginning or end of the book."

"That's considerate of her. Funny how publicity builds so differently with social media now. All the platforms that can be used to build buzz about an upcoming movie. Hash tags and all that."

Todd nodded. "It is. I'm interested in helping Alli publicize the movie in my blog. And especially promote the filming to tourists who come in. Every little bit helps."

I stopped Todd from touching the keyboard. "How hard is it to take a person out of a photo like Mandy's doing? Could I learn to do that?"

"Oh sure. If you wanted to learn. Even amateurs can edit photographs in programs like Photoshop. And the software has gotten so advanced that it's hard to even tell the photo has been retouched. Ready to see the video?"

Todd pressed a few keys and suddenly I was looking at me sitting at the computer. "This is the current view. Does it look right to you?"

"No. It needs to take in more of the gallery area. The security firm who set it up was adamant about getting the most area into the camera's view. Let's go back to the day before they came in and moved it. Then we'll know if it's even close to the same."

"Good idea," Todd said. "We can take a screenshot and compare."

The front door opening and Dennis Turner walking in interrupted us. My stomach knotted. I didn't want to chat with him now. I wanted to finish checking the camera and then head upstairs to get ready for my date with Scott.

"Quite the place you have here," Dennis said. "The transformation from the era we filmed is astounding." He clasped his hands behind his back as he strolled around the room checking the current photographic artists we had on display.

"Thanks Dennis," I said, hoping he'd get the hint that I was busy. "I'm wrapping up a couple things here."

"These seem to be other artists' work. Where is

yours, Jackie? I was hoping to buy a piece as a gift for my daughter."

Dennis may not have gotten my hint, but Todd did. "This way Mr. Turner. We'll be hanging Jackie's work back up soon. We moved them in back for the filming."

"Do I know you, young man?" Dennis asked.

"I'm Todd Baldwin, sir."

"Ah yes. Alli's friend. Nice to meet you. She's mentioned you. And very favorably!"

"That's good to hear. Right this way, sir."

"Before I go in back with this young man, I'd like to ask if you'd meet me for dinner tonight, Jackie, before we all pack up and leave town."

As I demurred, saying I already had plans, Todd moved back to the computer screen.

"Lucky guy. If you seriously can't change those plans, I'll leave tonight. Alli can handle reshooting the final scenes. I'm so proud of my baby for how hard she's worked and how quickly she learned. She has improved exponentially during this process. Too bad Marta messed with some of the scenes. It was a dastardly thing to do. I don't understand why. The digital changes she made were amateurish on top of it."

"Alli said there were actors taken out of scenes. Sort of what we were talking about, Jackie," Todd said. "Alli was crushed. Entire scenes might have to be cut out now. She couldn't believe Marta would do that to her or to Lewis."

"Is there anyone else who would want to see the project set back like this?" I asked Dennis.

"Why, would be my next question. To make Alli look bad? To ruin the film? This had been going on with other footage. Lewis, the cinematographer, was super pissed. Excuse my language," Dennis said. "Alli's always on my case about my word choices. Lewis knows his business and remembers how the shot was done, and Alli directed it fine. It had to be Marta."

"But you mentioned it looked amateurish. Todd said how easy it is to edit digital photographs and I would suppose then videos too."

"Might Wade himself have done it?" Todd suggested.

"That's not possible. He wanted this film to be the best it can."

"Even though he wasn't the head director?" Todd didn't look up from the computer screen.

"Something to think about," Dennis mused. "You're suggesting Marta's been taking the blame for the poorly edited film and all along Wade was messing with it?"

"It gives Marta motive if she knew it was him. Caught him in the act so to speak," I said.

Before he led Dennis to the back room to pick out a photograph, Todd said, "That film you wanted to see is close to the right time now, Jackie. Just go back to the exact date and time you need. Right this way, Mr. Turner."

I was glad Todd took him away. Now back to the computer screen to find that frame. I was getting close. This was cool. I saw them filming in here during the day. It was tempting to watch that, but I didn't have time now. Now I'm here, I am back to the first day of shooting. The camera caught the action on Main Street when they filmed my scene at Vogue on Main. I kept scrolling back, watching people walk backwards and cars move in reverse. Now I'm at the night Wade was murdered.

I slowed the rewind as a heaviness settled in my fingers.

I went forward several frames, keeping an eye on the date and time stamp.

I looked things over again. Then again.

When I heard Todd and Dennis coming back, I stopped and shut down the computer screen.

"Jackie, Mr. Turner picked out four of your prints he might like. He wanted your opinion though. And Alli just texted me. She's on her way!"

CHAPTER TWENTY-SIX

Dennis chose a photograph and a frame. I set up the shipping to Alli's home in LA and took Dennis' payment. I hurried not only because I wanted to get out of here, but because Alli would show up in a few minutes and he wanted it to be a surprise.

My thoughts went to a dark place. Would Alli be there when it arrived, or here in Harmony on trial for Wade's murder? Stop it, Jackie. She didn't do it. And now I have proof.

"Hey Dad, I didn't expect to see you," Alli said, shaking her umbrella out the front door before giving her father a quick hug. "What are you doing here? I hope you're not giving my aunt a hard time."

"Alli, where is your mind taking you? Jackie was just

showing me around the studio. Glad you're done with the Chief of Police."

"And I'm not arrested. At least not yet. But Patti said you wanted to see me, Jackie. What about?"

I didn't know how much to talk with her about her alibi in front of Todd and Dennis. She sensed my hesitation and said, "If it's about the murder, go ahead and ask. Todd and Dad have listened to me more than you can know. And I love them for it. But maybe a fresh view would help. I want you all to know that I'm a suspect in the murder of Wade Lambert."

Todd's eyes bugged out and Dennis gasped. Classic reactions to what was shocking news to them. Alli kept her eyes on me. Did she know what I'd done?

"Jackie, did you know about this? Is that why you asked me to come over?"

"Yes, I knew because I was the person who brought Jeff's attention to the error in the reported time of the gunshot. That change meant alibis needed verifying. I'm so sorry, Alli."

"Don't be sorry. Of course, you had to tell him. And even though my gun was stolen, Jeff has every right to suspect me." Alli looked toward her father. "I've been trying to remember just where I was. It was easy when it was around 8:20 p.m. because I was at the Stone Mill and lots of people saw me."

"Including me, sweetheart. What can I do to help? What is the new time you need an alibi for?"

"7:22 p.m. exactly. I forget just what time I got to the party. I had some calls while driving, including with Mom about her arrival. Then I got turned around and missed the place. But the calls don't cover the new time. And now, to top it off, Mom's telling me there are financial things that seem off." She held her head in her hands, her fingers massaging her temples.

"Maybe I shouldn't have rented separate cars for us," Dennis said. "She probably got hot about that."

Alli held up her hand. "Not now, Dad. Spare me that snarking between you two. Though that sports car was over the top. But I okayed it. I figured it was a small price to pay to have you onsite with me."

"But wasn't Wade approving charges too?" I asked.

"True. What a mess. But it'll work out somehow. The accountant is sending me the pertinent books to look over. Like I have time to do that while I'm here. We'll all be back in LA soon. I wish he'd just wait until then."

"Isn't your mother the producer?" Todd asked. "Doesn't that fall on her?"

"You're right," Dennis said. "And don't say I'm criticizing your mother again, but she should have been working with a better accountant."

"Todd, whisk me away from all this. Please!"

"You got it. See you all later," Todd said, his face beaming.

Kim entered just as they left. "Hey Alli, just the person I wanted to see. You look lovely. Is this young man treating you right? He's one of the good ones." Kim pulled her hood down and brushed the rain off her pastel plaid raincoat. "Do you have a second, Alli?"

"Sorry, Kim. Can't right now. But you know I'll be in town tomorrow to finish the reshoot. Maybe we can talk then. Bye bye." And with a quick wave the two ducked outside. Alli handed Todd her umbrella, and she took his elbow to hold them together under it.

"Well now, they were in a hurry," Kim said. "Hey Dennis, my husband Stu laughed himself silly when I told him about our forgery lesson. He said why did I even think I needed to know that? I told him I enjoy learning things. You never know what might come in handy. He said, don't get in trouble. When I explained how you had used the knowledge in *Bound for the West,* he was all about telling me what a great movie that was. And how much he loved hearing about all your research to make it authentic and..."

Dennis interrupted her words. "Please thank him from me. Now I also need to get going. It's been a pleasure meeting both of you ladies. Perhaps our paths will cross again someday." He did an arm across his waist bow and stepped out the door.

"What are you up to on this dreary rainy day Kim? By the way, I love the outfit." I turned to go back to my computer screen, curious to see if what I thought I saw was there before I was interrupted again.

"Can I share something with you, Jackie?"

"Well, I'm running behind…"

"Beverly Turner called and asked me to verify that all the lease agreements are up to date. She wants to make sure the checks have cleared the bank." Kim leaned in and with a conspiratorial voice said, "I think there's trouble brewing."

What had Kim uncovered? Was she thinking what I was? That the murder might have something to do with money?

"You okay?"

"Sure, I'm okay. Just under a time crunch," I said.

"No. Not okay like that. I meant money. Has Turner Production paid you? Val said she had to resubmit her payment. She laughed and said her bank never saw such a big check come into her account and they probably thought it wasn't real. Said she's no Keith Steele when it comes to money. He's super rich. Say did you know he's building a house on the bluff? Up near Scott's place, Val said. Val said that he hung out with you guys in high school. Then there was that issue with the credit card for those ball gowns. Did you hear about that?"

I rolled my eyes behind my computer screen where Kim couldn't see it. She could tangle up any conversation with her chatter. "I did get paid and Mandy confirmed our payment cleared the bank. Say, can I ask you something? Would you look at this video? I'm hoping you'll recognize something in it."

"Sure, I'd be happy to. Is it about the murder? I was wondering when you'd ask for my help. You usually do at some point. I love detective work."

Kim came around my desk to watch the video I'd pulled back up. But before I could even show it to her, she said, "Oh my. Look at this. He has the hots for you, Jackie. Should Scott be jealous?" She held up a note written on our shop notepad.

It was from Dennis. He'd left his phone number and the words *if you change your mind* with a heart drawn around his initials.

CHAPTER TWENTY-SEVEN

*A*fter making two phone calls I knew there was one more person to call before I went upstairs to freshen up.

I calmed my breathing before he picked up. "Hello, Dennis. It's Jackie."

"Jackie, what a pleasant surprise. Sorry I ducked out so soon. Does this call mean I should stop packing?"

"It does. I decided I'd like to take you up on that offer of dinner."

"Was it those sweet words I left on the notepad?"

I faked a giggle, hoping he believed it. "Sort of. I'm glad you left your phone number so I could reach you. Does the invite still stand?"

"It does. Can I pick you up in about an hour? I just got a call from your Chief of Police. He wants me to come to the station before I leave Harmony. Maybe to verify Alli's alibi?"

"Want me to come with you? I would like to, because I want to see what Jeff has on your daughter. Remember I'm related to her too."

"That's generous of you. I'd appreciate you coming along. Then we can go out afterwards. Perfect. I'll be over shortly."

Arriving at the police station with Dennis, I nearly fell over. There was Scott helping Eleana into the cab of his truck. He might not have noticed us, except Dennis made a point of calling Eleana's name.

Scott turned and saw me walking with Dennis Turner. My heart sank. Why does this keep happening?

Eleana looked like she'd been crying. Scott closed the truck door and approached us. "She's not feeling well. I don't think she wants to talk to anyone right now."

"Scott, this is Dennis Turner. Dennis, this is…"

"I know who he is, Jacqueline. Hope the two of you enjoy your evening. Jeff just told me he and Kay had to cancel tonight. Now I understand why." And with those words Scott strode back to his pickup and climbed in.

"I messed something up for you?"

"No. I did it all by myself." I could kick myself for not

letting Scott know I'd be a little late. But I'd been thinking about other things.

"I can't say I'm sorry if my taking you out did it," Dennis said. He held the door to the station open for me. "Let's get this over with and enjoy our evening together."

Beverly was seated in the waiting area when we arrived. "What are you doing here?" she asked.

"I could ask the same question, Bev."

Murph was behind the desk and Dennis asked if Jeff was available.

"Of course, sir. Are you Mr. Turner? He's expecting you. Please have a seat by your wife. The Chief would like to talk to both of you together."

"She's not my wife, and this is not what I expected. Ms. Parker and I have dinner plans. I'll come back later or tomorrow morning," Dennis said as he took my arm to leave.

I touched his hand. "I think we should stay. You might as well get this over rather than leave it hanging until morning. It might be good news."

"What is that supposed to mean? I'm not expecting something bad," he snapped back.

Well excuse me, I thought. I hadn't seen Dennis get short like that with anyone. He took me to the opposite side of the room. As far from Beverly as possible. "I'm sorry, Jackie. I didn't mean to snap. It's just that Bev brings that out in me. We can stay if it's alright with you."

"It is."

I watched seven uncomfortable minutes tick away on the wall clock before Murph stood and said Jeff was ready to see us now. "Is it okay if I come in with the Turners?"

Murph went back to check and said it would be fine. He led us into Jeff's office instead of one of the interview rooms.

"First, I want to say how much I appreciate you making yourself available on such short notice. This hasty meeting was called for a couple of reasons. The discovery that the person who heard the gunshot gave us the wrong time jolted our timeline. As you might expect, that put a twist in our investigation. It did eliminate one suspect, which I'm sure she was happy about. You may have seen her leaving. But it left us having to reinterview some other people of interest."

"Meaning my daughter?" Beverly leaned forward in her seat, resting her arms on a briefcase on her lap.

"Yes. Of course. It's probable that her gun was the murder weapon. I spent time with her this afternoon," Jeff said. He pulled a file out and shuffled through the papers in it.

No one spoke.

Jeff kept his head down, as though intent on finding something in the papers spread in front of him.

Finally, Beverly said, "And…why are we both here? Are you going to tell us our daughter is being charged with murder? You told me you wanted further information on the apparent mishandling of funds. Has that changed?"

"No. Is that what you brought along in that briefcase?"

"Yes. I had my accountant send the data to me and the resort printed up copies. But I'd rather my ex-husband not be here for all of it. As producer of the movie, it is my job to handle the money. He has no formal role in this and should not be privy to how my money is spent."

Beverly opened her briefcase. "I do, however want to bring up one point Mr. Turner needs to be made aware of." She pulled a manila file folder out and reached to put it on the desktop.

"In that folder are initialed purchase orders and authorized expenditures. I approved both my daughter and Wade to initial such paperwork and forward it to the accountant. Wade initialed the highlighted items. But if you look closely some of them appear to be forged."

"Oh really? I didn't expect such a quick result to your inquiries. Perhaps this plays more of a role than I first thought." Jeff took the folder and began running his finger down a column of numbers and notes.

The wood encased wall clock ticked softly.

"Why did you conclude these are not Mr. Lambert's initials?"

Beverly narrowed her eyes as she looked at Dennis. "My ex was very entertaining with stories involving his directorial efforts. I don't know how many times he told the story about studying forgeries when he directed *Bound for the West.*"

I didn't flinch, but Dennis did. From the corner of my eye, I saw his hands clench.

"Those initials are different enough to suggest they aren't Wade's." Beverly leaned back.

"Go on, Mrs. Turner. I feel you have more to share," Jeff said, his fingertips resting on the paperwork.

"I also know the person who did it because I've seen his signature hundreds of times. Including the initialing of corrections on realty contracts and divorce papers."

CHAPTER TWENTY-EIGHT

*A*ll eyes turned toward Dennis.

"I don't know if I can lay much blame on the accountant for letting these initialed expenditures go through," Beverly said. "At a quick glance, these look like Wade's initials, but they aren't. When my ex-husband initialed things, he always included his middle initial, L for Laurence. In several of these I see the familiar dropped loop he used in the L for Lambert."

"Seriously, Bev?" Dennis said. "A loop? Wade used a loop too. You're stretching the facts to account for your own failures."

Beverly continued to hold her eyes on Dennis, whose right foot was now rapidly tapping.

"The first initials you forged were excellent. But then

as time went on, you got sloppy, darling. I use the same accountant for my personal things. He's the one who pointed it out to me just today. He questioned Wade a few days ago. But before Wade could respond, he was gone. Did he say he'd lie for you? In return for what, Dennis?"

"How dare you imply I would do something like that to my own daughter?"

"But don't you see? You weren't doing it to her. You were doing it to me," Beverly said in a firm voice. "Admit that much, Dennis. After all, these were not enormous expenses. Pocket money really. You got your fun out of sticking it to me."

I could hear the gears turning in Dennis's brain. Smart on Beverly's part. I knew what he was thinking. They hadn't found everything he embezzled.

"If you pay me back within ten business days, I'll not press charges," Beverly said.

It didn't take Dennis long to confess. He admitted he may have done it a few times. That it was a revenge move for everything the divorce cost him. He agreed to Beverly's terms.

"Well now, that veered off track," Jeff said. "Not what I was expecting, but it sounds like you two have reached an agreement. What I called you in for was to let you know I am focused on Marta and may charge her with the murder. I wanted you both to find out so you can relax. Alli will not be charged."

Beverly put on a marvelous performance. She even ran and threw her arms around Dennis. He hesitated before returning the hug.

"She's cleared. I can't believe it. I was all set to hear it was Alli. She didn't have an alibi, and it was her gun," Beverly said, beaming at Dennis.

Dennis, now relaxed, praised Jeff. "Good investigative techniques. Marta never had an alibi, did she? Whichever time the murder occurred. But why on earth would she shoot Wade?"

"Simple. Wade resented Alli getting the director's job. He told others it was his. When Alli was brought in, he began to sabotage her."

"By messing with scenes already shot!" Dennis said.

"That's right. It would be too expensive to go back to Florida or New York and reshoot them. Your daughter would end up looking like a bad director. It was motive enough because when Marta caught on to it and confronted Wade, he threatened to throw her under the bus. She'd get blamed. He didn't care who he took out, who he stepped on to get to the top." Jeff paused to let it all sink in.

But the surprises weren't over. I knew where this

was going to end up, but what Jeff said next both surprised and pleased me.

"Perhaps you saw Eleana leaving the station just now. She was here to tell me something. She confirmed Wade was angry and bitter about not getting the head director position. That it was eating him up and he said he'd make the Turners pay."

"That bum! Job well done, Chief. I'm grateful to Bev for giving me a few days to compensate her so I won't be charged with financial fraud. And thankful that now I can take this lovely lady out to dinner," Dennis said as he stood.

"One more thing, Mr. Turner. Where did you say you were between 7:15 and 7:30 p.m. the night of the murder?"

"I was at the Stone Mill gathering by then." Dennis reached for my hand. "Shall we get going?"

"Hmm. I seem to remember someone say you apologized for being late. That was you, Jackie. That it was shortly before eight when you showed up. Close to the time Alli got there."

"What are you implying, Officer?" Dennis tilted his head and narrowed his eyes.

"If you'd like time to think over your answer, you can have it. But by the security video sent to me just this afternoon, I'd say you should weigh your answer carefully."

CHAPTER TWENTY-NINE

sat on the bench in front of my studio with Libby resting at my feet. Since the cameras were aimed on the other side of the street this morning, they had given Val the go ahead to open the salon up. She stopped by to say hi and confirmed what Kim had told me yesterday. Our old high school buddy Keith was moving here and building a house on the bluff near Scott's place. It would be fun to see him again.

Beverly sat by my side on the bench. Last night she'd held it together, pulling out her acting chops to get through the scene I'd suggested to her and Jeff.

"I must thank you again for your help last night, Beverly. Do you have any idea yet just how much Dennis absconded with?"

She shook her head. "I don't. But from what Eleana

told Jeff, enough for Wade to be on easy street for keeping his mouth shut. So sad. Dennis became a bitter man over the past years. His career was slipping away, but he couldn't admit it. I'm still in shock that it would have gone this far though. Wade had his own issues, but nothing to be killed for."

"Dennis thought differently. He didn't want his cover blown. And what fortuitous timing that Eleana told Jeff about Wade's threats to reveal the embezzling," I said. "It confirmed everything."

Beverly chuckled. "I admit I was impressed with the extent of what Dennis did. Of course, I didn't pull that all out last night. I wanted to throw him off."

"Very clever of you. He relaxed and thought that it was settled. But you really kicked it up a notch when you went and hugged Dennis. I almost started laughing. Maybe you should try directing?"

"As to your question about how much he'd embezzled, my accountant is still working through the layers, like discovering front companies who'd work with Dennis on cleaning up the money trail. Wonder if he perpetrated this fraud on other production companies?"

Jeff would be charging Dennis with murder. The film crew would leave town and we could get back to our day-to-day lives. But then I remembered Scott hadn't answered my calls last night. He didn't hear my explanation about what I was doing to keep Dennis in town, like faking a dinner date with him. Jeff promised to reach Scott and explain, but I don't know if he succeeded.

Mandy came bouncing up. "Good morning, Jackie. Mrs. Turner. Nice to see the sun out again and be back at work. My students will be happy to know our regular class schedule resumes. I just got that new framing material and I'm excited to see how it looks with that seasonal series of photographs you took, Jackie."

"You mean the ones out across the lake? Or the solitary tree series?"

"I'm thinking first the lake. Summer tourists will be very attracted to them. Especially since you shot them from the high point on the resort grounds."

Mandy left to open up for the day.

Rod Jessup, dressed as Judge Josiah Bell, waved from the door of Vogue on Main. Dionne came across the street to say a quick hello to Beverly. My mother would have loved the ripe peach colored sheath she was wearing for her scene.

"Jackie, how did you get the video of Dennis driving by? That was a big clue," Beverly said.

I turned and pointed up at my security camera inside the studio. "Your crew bumped it during their work here. That meant the past couple of days the camera was misaligned. It filmed Main Street instead of the studio's interior. I wanted to get it back to the original angle. While scrolling back in the video to find that time, I had to return to before the night of the murder."

"And you saw Dennis in that silly and expensive sports car he rented. How very fitting! Did he think no one would notice him?"

"I suppose he parked behind the Village Hall. Maybe Dennis didn't plan a murder but was going to straighten things up with Wade? He had to be getting desperate," I said.

"But the gun. Why would he have the gun?" Beverly said. "It had to be premeditated. He was in and out of Alli's room talking business. Easy enough for him to grab it."

"Good point, Beverly. How's Alli doing?"

"Not good. We'll talk more soon. She just wanted to keep this quiet until we leave town, and I think she's accomplishing that. No one brought it up to me today. Excuse me, I'm going to use your restroom before I go join Alli. I just wanted to come by and let you know how much the effort you took to protect Alli means to me."

"She's my niece. I'd do anything for her. And for you, Beverly."

Val came back from her studio. "Can you believe it? Dennis Turner committed murder!"

"You don't say. Where did you get that information from?" I asked.

"Me!" Kim said, as she followed behind Val.

I started laughing. Harmony was certainly getting back to normal. The gossip mills were clicking along just as usual.

CHAPTER THIRTY

unt Ruth joined me in goodbye hugs for Alli and Beverly. We assured them that we both looked forward to seeing the finished movie. Big waves and horn honks were exchanged as the trailers pulled out of town. Hannah and Mark had Sutton Antiques open. Val's customers were glad to get back in her salon chairs. Mandy's class was already working with the new framing material she'd received.

A walk along the river bluffs east of Harmony was just the therapy I needed now.

I loaded up my backpack with water and the new treats I'd ordered for Libby. She had my number regarding getting treats during training. "There will be a new ratio going forward," I cautioned her. "I've been a pushover for you. That's done."

The back end of the Stone Mill parking lot would be a good point to join the Mary-Go-Round trail. I'd go past the marina storage toward the back edge of Shady Pines where the trail split. To the left it climbed up the hills into the farmlands above town. To the right the bluff trail began its ascent to cliffs above the river. With my backpack on, my camera hung from a strap around my neck, and Libby by my side, I started out.

Besides a way to clear my head, my decision to hike the bluff trail as opposed to the Mary-Go-Round trail was that it passed near Scott's house. It was beyond time to straighten things out with him. My timing was based on when I thought Scott would be home from work. He might see through my ruse, but I'd deal with that.

Fresh pine needle scents wafted up. The crisp cleanness of the air in these evergreens never ceased to amaze me. Days were getting longer, and the sun was still comfortably high on the horizon. I'd have time before twilight descended.

I let Libby run loose. She'd been doing good with grasping how far she could stray, before returning when I called her back. We'd barely gotten going when she bolted into the forest. I gave her time to explore before whistling for her.

She didn't come. I didn't count on this happening. I should have leashed her until we were further from the brewery and the parking lot. I'm sure there were tempting scents for her to follow here.

I called in a more demanding tone and heard her coming back through the underbrush. When I saw what she carried in her mouth, I said, "Well now, my canine friend. Two treats for you."

I sent out a quick group text to Patti and Jeff including the photo of Libby sitting proudly, waiting to receive her treat, the key to Village Hall still hanging from her mouth.

Was the gun tossed away here too? I decided to let Jeff search for that on his own.

As the bluff trail continued climbing above the river, the views expanded. My love of photography slowed me down as I bent to get closeups of the trilliums and wood violets scattered in the surrounding forest. I was careful not to trip on a root or a rock as I looked between trunks of the tall white pines for spots to photograph the river far below.

Scott's house sat above the trail so I couldn't see in his windows from this angle. I knew that not far ahead the trail came closer to the top of the bluff. There I could leave the trail and cut through to the road. If I happened to cut the angle and ended near his house instead, well, I could blame Libby.

Better yet, I'd go check out the site where our former

classmate Keith was building. It would be closer to the trail and a believable reason for wandering around up here. On the last leg of the trail's climb to the top I saw where land was being cleared. That must be the future spot of the Steele home.

Suddenly Libby began running toward the clearing. She saw Scott before I did. This worked out perfectly. I was close to the clearing as Libby let out happy yips and Scott turned, surprised to see her bounding out. That's when I saw the wine glass in his hand and a young woman on the other side of him. She held a wine glass too. I kept a smile frozen on my face and willed my legs to keep walking toward them.

Libby continued her barking as Scott teased her. She loved him. She lay down on her front paws, her rear end wiggling, taunting him. He lunged. She leaped back. A game they often played.

"Well, this is a surprise," I said, having already planned a cover for my being here on the bluff. "Libby and I were enjoying a hike, and I heard about our classmate building a house somewhere up here. But I can see you're not Keith." The words sounded stupid as they echoed in my head. Enough. Close your mouth, Jackie.

"You're right. I'm not Keith." A friendly look crossed her face. "But he is my husband. I'm Tara and you found the right spot."

Scott lowered his wine glass, moving it to his side as though I hadn't seen it. "Tara, this is Jacqueline Parker."

"Keith has mentioned you being a classmate," Tara said as she moved her glass to her left hand in order to offer a handshake to me. "I'll have to tell him we met."

"We were just going over the layout of the house," Scott said.

"That's nice. Do you have the blueprint with you?" I wondered what layout he was talking about. This looks like a pile of cut trees and brush.

Tara replied as she stepped closer to Scott. "The plans are back at the house. I asked him to bring me over here to see the view with the trees cleared."

"Nice." She must have seen my questioning glance at the wine bottle and small tray of cheese and crackers on a nearby stump.

"Oh that. I wanted to share a toast to our journey together. So, Scott kindly grabbed a wine from his place, and we walked along the road to get here. And thank you for suggesting bringing the cheese," Tara said as she smiled up at Scott. "I think I'll like Wisconsin more than I thought."

"Okay then. I'd better get going. Enjoy your wine and cheese. Scott has learned a great deal about wine since I've known him. I'm sure he picked the perfect bottle for you."

I snapped Libby's leash on and began walking back to the trail. Scott came hurrying after me.

"Wait, Jackie. This isn't what you think. I'm building a house for them."

"Well then, I guess we're even in the isn't-what-it-looks-like world. I've got to hurry so I don't lose the light."

Scott reached for my hand. "Jackie, you're seeing me with a client and making it something more. You stood me up three times for him."

"I did not. Oh, forget it. We'll talk later."

"No. This has to be cleared up here and now."

Tara called out. "Scott? Are you coming back? I'm not sure I can find my way back to your house alone."

"Mrs. Steele needs help. You like being a white knight. You swooped in and took the sad, crying Eleana out on your trusty pontoon boat on the lake. Now wine and cheese with a client's wife. Let me know when you have time for me. Or at least when you can return my messages."

"Jeff tried explaining what happened last night. I didn't want to hear him. But now I know I over reacted. I'm sorry." Scott pulled my hand to his lips. "I'll walk her back to the house and she can leave from there. Will you please come up to the house with us?"

"My SUV is down by the Stone Mill. I'll think about it on the walk back."

"I'll be waiting for you on the deck with a fire going."

I squeezed his hand and pulled away. "Come on, Libby. Time to go."

The End

If you enjoyed Digital Deception a review would be very much appreciated. Whether with written comments or simply as a starred review, it is something that will help future readers find the series.

ABOUT THE AUTHOR

Here are a few ways to reach me...I'd love to stay connected!

Please <u>sign up for my monthly newsletter</u>. I'll share things about my life...both personal as Brenda Felber and professionally as my pen name Suzanne Bolden.
Like/follow Suzanne on her Facebook page

If you follow me on these two, you'll be automatically notified when new releases are available.
Bookbub
<u>Amazon Author Central</u>

Check out my website <u>www.suzannebolden.com</u>

Thank you for reading my books. If you enjoyed them, a review is much appreciated!

ALSO BY SUZANNE BOLDEN

Katie Murphy Cozy Mystery Series

#1 Pour Decisions

#2 Pick Yar Poison

#3 Raising Spirits

#4 Auld Lang Stein

#5 A Wee Lepre-Con

#6 Paws for a Pint

7 The Elf Did It

#8 Matrimony and Malice

#9 Read Between the Lines

ALSO BY SUZANNE BOLDEN

Parker Photography Cozy Mystery

#1 Captured on Camera

#2 Murder in a Dark Gloom

#3 Focus on Fraud

#4 An Appraisal to Die For

#5 A Filmsy Excuse

#6 A Negative Result

#7 Framed for Murder

#8 Digital Deception

#9 A Developing Attraction

#10 Skewered Perspective

#11 A Killer Shot

#12 Holiday Havoc

Series completed

9 781948 064316